Texas Wildflower

To,
Heather

Texas Wildflower

by

Debra L. Hall

Debra L. Hall

authorHOUSE®

AuthorHouse™
1663 Liberty Drive
Bloomington, IN 47403
www.authorhouse.com
Phone: 1-800-839-8640

Published by AuthorHouse   08/30/2011

ISBN: 978-1-4567-6977-2 (sc)

Printed in the United States of America

Any people depicted in stock imagery provided by Thinkstock are models, and such images are being used for illustrative purposes only.
Certain stock imagery © Thinkstock.

This book is printed on acid-free paper.

Cover Illustration: Bruce Bealmear and Stephen Getzschman for the title page drawing.
First printing by Capper's Press, Topeka, Kansas, August 1996 - Second printing: revised by the author 2011

Special thanks to my husband, Robert Hall to Larry Carter, Bob Bodmer and to Connie Sanchez for their assistance in the reproduction of this book.

Dedicated to Theresa

For giving me Texas

Chapter One

"*I* know it was wrong. I should have told you the truth years ago, but no matter how hard I tried, I . . . I just couldn't. There were so many painful memories."

Violet Tippon's thoughts were interrupted by the long wailing call of the train's whistle, causing her to blink back the startling images of a lonely past that kept flashing through her mind. She stared blankly at the countryside whizzing by. Clackety, clackety, clack, the sound of the train teetering along the tracks distracted her.

If only her mother had told the truth about her father. Instead, she let Violet live with the carefully fashioned memories of a caring father who had died in a tragic accident. Violet sighed as she opened the drawstring on her black worsted bag and pulled out a worn envelope.

Although the letter about her father suffering a stroke arrived only three days ago, it seemed weeks since she had quarreled with her mother, Violet insisting that she be allowed to go to Texas to find her father.

"You'll never come back," her mother had cried from the bed where she lay in a mound of down quilts and fluffed pillows.

Aunt Tilly had been bustling about the room, preparing a bath for her sister and straightening this and that when all at once she stopped, her eyes full of concern, her lips pursed tightly.

"Your mother's right. You're only eighteen. You should be going to parties and luncheons and such with your friends." Her aunt picked up the feather duster. "It's time you took more of an interest in a few of the gentlemen who have been calling, instead of traipsing across the country after a dying man's dream."

As her aunt left the room with the rattling dinner tray, she had added an unmistakable huff at the end of a trail of "should haves" where Violet's father was concerned.

Violet remembered having waited for a moment, in case her aunt should decide to open the door and insist that she take her advice, the way she usually did. After a brief silence, Violet had leaned toward the bed. Her eyes filled with ready tears, she confided in her mother.

"All I want to do is see him and hear his voice. After all, he is my father."

Violet's mother turned her face away, dabbing her eyes with a lace-trimmed handkerchief.

"I wanted to tell you," she wept, "but I just couldn't. Most of the time, I didn't even know where he was, or if he was even alive. If it hadn't been for the money your grandfather left me, I don't know what we would have done. Where would we have lived if your Aunt Tilly hadn't shared her house with us?"

"Didn't Father ever send you any money?" Violet asked.

"At first he did. Then time passed, and I seldom heard from him. Every year I wrote; and I sent photographs of you, but there was never a reply."

Violet had struggled with their conflicting emotions. "That's why I need to go," she pleaded. "I need to find out why he stayed away."

"But Violet, you don't understand. That's rough country, with desperate outlaws. It's no place for a young woman to go alone."

"But I won't be alone. Hattie's promised to go with me."

"Hattie! Why she's nearly 70 years old!"

"Then you can be sure there won't be anything to worry about."

Violet's shoulders sagged when she recalled how her mother had sighed heavily and slumped down into the pillows.

Now, struggling with the contents of the letter, Violet reminded herself that her mother was still not well. That winter, she had been weakened by a fever and cough that refused to let up.

Nonetheless, Violet had to go to Texas. She felt betrayed by this long-withheld secret, especially now that her father was on the verge of death. All she had to remind herself of him was a cracked and faded photograph of a grizzled old man. He hardly resembled the tall, handsomely clad stranger in the small photograph pressed in her mother's locket, which her mother had kept hidden in a drawer in her bedroom.

After much debate, and assurance that Hattie, the housekeeper, would accompany her, Violet had somehow managed to convince her mother, and aunt, that she should go to Wood River, Texas, to meet her dying father. She had promised to return as soon as possible.

*   *   *

Violet, startled by a sudden jar of the train, glanced at Hattie, who was sound asleep. Her own tired eyes closed tightly against burning tears. Going to Texas was something she had to do. She wanted to feel the place where her father had lived after he went away. There must have been something strongly appealing about Wood River and the Tangleweed Ranch that could keep a man from those who loved and needed him.

The long day finally ended at a small, run-down hotel in a shabby town that remained nameless in Violet's mind. Violet dragged their valises up two flights of rickety stairs and down a dark, narrow hallway to what appeared to be more of a closet than a room for paying guests. The only window had been painted shut, so there was no way to let in fresh air, it being an unusually warm night.

Violet sat up most of the night fanning Hattie, who tossed in fitful sleep on a narrow cot. Violet dozed off and on until dawn when Hattie reached out and grasped her forearm.

"Go on without me. Find your father." Hattie's voice crackled.

Violet's eyes flew open. "Hattie! What's wrong?"

"I don't have the strength to go on," the old woman said.

"Just rest now. You'll feel better later," Violet reassured, trying not to let Hattie hear the alarm she felt.

Hattie withdrew her hand, and Violet stirred uneasily in her chair. Later, as the window paled with light, Violet looked down at Hattie and realized her companion was gone.

Numbly coming to grips with reality, Violet stayed behind when the train pulled out of the station a few hours later. She wanted to care for her beloved housekeeper.

With trembling fingers, she dressed Hattie and packed her meager belongings before the local undertaker came and took her away. Violet paid a goodly sum to have Hattie's body sent back to St. Louis, then made her way to the telegraph office where she sent a message to her mother.

Violet explained what had happened and assured her mother that she was all right.

She had reason to doubt that statement when she stepped outside the hotel the next morning. She gasped and stumbled backwards until the only thing holding her up was the wall. Across the street a man was hanging from a scaffold that hadn't been there the night before.

"Round here, we hang rustlers and horse thieves, ma'am. There ain't no other language they understand."

Violet shuddered, her heart pounding in her ears. The deep, gravely sound of the cowboy's voice had left its effect upon her. She raised her eyes slowly, watching the tall, angular man stride down the boardwalk, his spurs jingling as every step threw his greatcoat open.

Shivering, she clutched her bag with one hand, her throat with the other, and hurried toward the depot, only too aware of the taut rope squeaking as the lifeless body swayed eerily in the stiff breeze.

The whistle blew sharply as Violet boarded the train. She blinked away the vivid image and covered her trembling lips with the back of her gloved hand. She swallowed hard. Although she was bone weary from traveling and lack of sleep, she was determined not to cry again. She reminded herself that at least now she knew what she was up against. The only thing that kept her from turning back was the thought of seeing her father. She had to learn the truth about why he left.

Once seated, Violet again removed the worn envelope from her bag. Shakily she unfolded the creased paper, and read what represented the only tangible link she had ever had with her father.

To Miss Violet Tippon:

It is with deep regret that I sit down to write this here letter to tell you your pa had a stroke on Friday the tenth day in May of 1889. He told me if he should die, you, his one and only daughter, should have his ranch known in these parts as Tangleweed. You are welcome to stay with us at the Rough and Tumble Ranch if you should decide to come to Wood River. Your pa asked me to send this here picture of him taken when he was in San Francisco a few years back.

Friends of your Pa, Ruth and Ben Tridel

Stuffing the letter into the envelope, Violet sniffed back the urge to cry. A month ago, her father was the furthest thing from her mind, and now she was on her way to Texas, clinging to a tattered picture and a vision of a piece of wild country called Tangleweed.

* * *

"Sander's Creek up ahead. Everybody off at Sander's Creek."

Above the low groan of overwrought passengers, Violet, waving her hand to stop the conductor, called out, "Sir!" He turned at the sound of her voice, and she rose slightly from the horsehair seat. "Sir, isn't this train supposed to go to Wood River, Texas?"

The conductor balanced himself between the rows of dusty seats as he retraced his teetering steps. "You from St. Louis, ma'am?"

Violet offered a pleasant, reassuring nod.

"I guess the dad gum telegram didn't get through in time. This here's the last stop. The tracks are out five miles outside of Sander's Creek."

"But how will I get to Wood River?"

"Wood River?"

"I was supposed to go to Wood River, Texas."

The conductor eyed the ticket stubs in his hand. "I don't know, ma'am. But you can show 'em this here ticket stub, and I reckon they'll give you part of your money back."

With a disconcerted look on her face, Violet lamented, "But I don't want my money back. I sent a telegram. People are expecting me in Wood River this evening. It's important that I arrive on time."

"No disrespect intended, ma'am, but out in these parts, folks expect a lot, and when they don't get what they expect, they just go on expectin' till their hopes run dry. So, I wouldn't fret none if I was you. Today's no different than any other day as far as waitin' goes. I guarantee you they'll be there waitin' for you on Saturday the same as they'd be waitin' any other day of the week."

"But how . . ."

"I reckon you could take the stagecoach, ma'am. There'll be one headed to Wood River in the mornin'."

The wailing train whistle was followed by the sound of screeching brakes and a sudden jolt that sent Violet sprawling into the corner of her seat. Her elbow-length cape flew up over the back of her head, and her once carefully placed hat now hid her flushed face while she frantically fought to manage her disheveled skirts.

"Is there anything I can do to help, ma'am?" a voice drawled from a height near the arched ceiling of the boxcar.

Flustered, Violet scrambled to an upright position, fumbling with her hat until she saw the broad silhouette of a man framed against the light coming through the windows. "No, thank you," she blurted. "I can take care of myself."

By the time Violet had gained her composure, all that was left of the tall, dark stranger was a fleeting glimpse of a wide-brimmed Stetson disappearing through the narrow door and into the glaring afternoon sun.

It was close to sundown when Violet entered the only available hotel in Sander's Creek, hoping to secure a room for the night.

"I would like to have a bath sent to my room, please," she said in a weary voice as she bent down and gripped her floral valise.

The bearded man behind the counter frowned, his thin lips clamped tightly for a perplexed moment. Then he scratched his crooked jaw and said, "I'm sorry, ma'am, but baths are only available on Saturday night."

"What?" Violet looked at his bushy brows folded over his eyes.

"We gotta pay someone to haul the water in, so we only . . ."

"Oh! never mind." Violet dropped her shoulders with a disgruntled sigh. "Is there any way I can have a basin of water sent to my room?"

The clerk nodded obligingly. "Sure. That'll cost ya' four bits."

"Four bits?" Violet frowned.

"Fifty cents, ma'am."

"Fifty cents!" Violet gasped, her voice filled with disbelief. "I suppose if I want something to eat, that would be out of the question, too?"

The man motioned toward the door. "A plate of food'd cost ya' 'bout a dollar down at the Broken Rail."

"The Broken Rail? What's that?"

"It's a saloon just down the street a ways. They serve up real good food, and it don't take long, neither."

"A saloon!" Violet dropped her valise with a thump and promptly slapped the man's face. "How dare you insinuate that I would enter a saloon!"

Just then, the door opened and the large figure of a man carrying a saddle on his shoulder filled the dimly lit entrance. Violet spun around and noticed right away that the man wore a gun belt. The butt of his pistol was longer than the span of his hand. She was unable to see the man's face beneath the shadow of his wide-brimmed hat, but she recognized the drawl when he spoke to the hotel clerk, who was rubbing the red spot on his cheek.

"I see you've been making friends again, Jake."

The clerk groaned and gave Violet a perturbed look. "Ma'am, this here's Sander's Creek; it ain't no big city. The only way you're gonna eat tonight is if I order you a plate of food, and they send someone over with it."

Violet squared her shoulders, forcing her attention away from the stranger who had crossed the room and now towered beside her at the counter. "I guess that'll have to do," she replied, digging rapidly through her bag in search of her coin purse.

"You got a room for the night, Jake?" the cowboy asked matter-of-factly.

"Sure." The clerk turned and lifted a key from a nail on the wall behind him, placing it on the scarred countertop. "Did ya' have a long haul this time out?"

The stranger slid a few coins out of his vest pocket and tossed them onto the counter. He waited until they stopped spinning before he hoisted his saddle on his shoulder and turned toward the stairs. "Not bad. Couple hundred steers. Got a decent price for the herd, and the boys are all paid up. No one's complainin'." He stopped midway up the stairs and, looking back at Violet, he tipped his hat with his free hand. "Don't be too hard on ol' Jake. He ain't used to waitin' on a lady."

Feeling the heat rising in her cheeks, Violet turned away from the cowboy's twinkling eye. Mother was right, she thought to herself. This country's full of rough men and coarse ways. If only Hattie . . . . But there was no turning back now. If she was really as stubborn as her father, the way her mother always said she was, then she would make it to Wood River, even if she had to walk the rest of the way.

*　　*　　*

The sound of loud banging on the door startled Violet. She sprang upright in the sagging bed, clutching the coarse blanket beneath her chin.

"Stage is leavin' in 15 minutes."

"Fifteen minutes!" she cried out.

"Sorry, ma'am, it came early. It's the last one out today."

"Ohhh!" Violet groaned. She jumped from the bed, tearing off her night-gown, which she tossed into her open valise. She scurried into her corset, only halfway managing the ties. She finally gave up, slipped into her camisole and jumped into her ruffled petticoat and fitted blouse. She pulled her skirt down over her dangling auburn curls to her waist before she tugged on her waistcoat, which she partly buttoned to hide her rumpled blouse. She stuffed the remainder of her belongings into her valise, then catching a glimpse of her flushed face in the mirror, she cried, "This'll never do."

A man's voice bellowed up the stairs. "Five minutes."

Violet hurriedly pulled on her boots then grabbed her valise and cape. Taking a quick look around the room, she snatched up her hat and two hat boxes, jerked open the door, and clattered noisily down the stairs. Her haphazard state of dress seemed of little importance until she saw the astonished look on the clerk's face when she stopped at the bottom of the stairs. She fought to catch her breath while struggling into her gloves. She remained speechless, her hand clamped tightly to her mismanaged waistcoat. Having somewhat gained her composure she looked up.

"There was so little time. I . . . I . . ."

"You best save your explainin' for later, ma'am," the clerk said, as he quickly made his way around the counter to open the door.

"Thank you. Thank you so much. Oh, I . . . I'm sorry for slapping you last night. I . . ."

"Forget it. I figured you was just practicin' up."

A quizzical look flashed over Violet's face before she was hustled out the door and pointed in the direction of the departing stagecoach.

The burly driver, who was covered from head to foot in a greatcoat and broad Stetson, was just climbing to the driver's seat when she called for him to wait. He stopped dead in his tracks and eyed her openly.

"You sure you're ready to go, lady?"

Violet stopped, her lips pursed to keep herself from apologizing again. She was quite unaccustomed to having men stare at her in such a bold and all-out fashion. She pulled her dragging cape over her arm.

"Yes, I'm quite ready," she said with as much confidence as she could muster.

She looked at the dark windows of the coach and took a deep breath to calm her frazzled nerves. From what she could see, it looked empty. She was thankful for that. It had been a hectic week. She welcomed some time alone to think.

With a heavy sigh of relief, she looked at the driver, who tipped his head back just far enough to spit a stream of tobacco juice through the gap between his front teeth that showed beneath his long, bushy mustache. Before she had time to consider the queasiness in her stomach, he walked over, took her valise and hat boxes, and tossed them on top of the coach. She protested, following close on his heels to the opposite side of the coach. It was no use, however. He didn't pay an ounce of attention to her until he stopped and offered to help her into the stagecoach. She smiled and placed her hand into his gloved one, then let out a cry of alarm when she was all but tossed into the open cavity of the enormous coach. The door slammed shut so the driver couldn't hear the names she called him as she scrambled to a sitting position.

She grunted, sweeping her tangled hair from her face, only to find herself sitting across from the same cowboy who had so enormously silhouetted the open doorway at the hotel.

"It appears you're not used to getting up at sunrise," he said in a voice as smooth as molasses.

With a loud shout and the crack of a whip, the coach lunged forward, filling the compartment with a cloud of dust. Violet went sprawling across the wide seat, her hand covering her mouth as she coughed back the dust that quickly settled. With her free arm outstretched, she frantically fought to keep herself from falling forward onto the stranger's lap. It wasn't until the coach had settled into a steady rocking motion that she realized her bodice was in an even worse state of disarray than when she left the Hotel.

"It appears to me, sir," she said, fumbling nervously with the tiny buttons, "that you are not in the habit of treating a woman like a lady."

"I thought about offering some assistance, but, well, I figured that was something you could probably handle by yourself." He indicated what he had in mind by nodding toward her disorderly clothing.

Violet huffed, swatting at a curl that persistently bobbed over her brow. "The least you could do is look the other way while I . . ." Groaning in frustration, she turned her head, refusing to mention any particulars.

"I'm sorry, ma'am, but it's hard not to stare at a pretty lady, since there are so few in these parts."

Violet found it hard to believe that she looked pretty in the state she was in. "Well, if you have to stare then do it later."

"I'll take you up on that, hopin', of course, you won't change your mind when the time comes." Without waiting for her to reply, the man pulled his gun from his holster and rapped loudly on the ceiling of the coach.

Startled, Violet gasped and fell back against the seat, hoping beyond hope that the gun being so freely wheeled about wasn't loaded.

She heard a loud "Whoa!" and the stagecoach slowed down. Before it completely halted, the long-legged cowboy flung open the door, swung outside and into the first strong rays of sunlight, kicked the door shut behind him and disappeared. Violet heard a loud thump and realized that he was on top of the stagecoach with the driver.

All at once Violet felt, what energy she had left, drain from her body. She slumped down in the gritty seat, tears falling from her tired eyes.

"This wasn't supposed to happen," she muttered in a weak, defeated voice. "I'll probably arrive and nobody will be there."

Violet sniffed loudly, wiping away her tears. She dragged her tired body toward the edge of the seat and turned at the waist until she was facing the corner. Slowly, mechanically, she unbuttoned her waistcoat and blouse. She untangled the strings on her camisole then straightened her corset and laced up her camisole properly. When she was finished buttoning her blouse and waistcoat, Violet turned around. Without thinking about her hair or her unlaced boots, she pulled her cloak over her shoulders and closed her eyes.

She wouldn't fall asleep. She just wanted to rest a while.

All at once, Violet cried out, bolting upright in her seat. White lightning had cut the darkened sky in two, followed by a growing thunder that seemed to rise out of the bowels of the vast, empty wasteland. For a moment, she was blinded by streak after streak of jagged lightning that splintered the sky like the fine lines on her aunt's cracked china. With her hands clenched tightly together, she prayed, wondering for a forbidden moment if it would do her any good in this godforsaken country.

"Whoa! Whoa there, ol' Blue. Come on, Babe. Whoa!" the driver's brusque voice bellowed.

Violet fell toward the window, her eyes fixed on the dark, rumbling sky overhead. As far as she could see, there was nothing but a few trees dotting the open country. "What kind of place is Texas?" she wondered aloud.

The stagecoach continued to rock violently from side to side, like a ship on a stormy sea. Her body ached and her ribs felt bruised. Her fears were further intensified when an enormous bolt of lightning rent apart the clouds and thrust a wicked streak toward a lone tree a short distance away. It slashed the boughs from the trunk as though they were twigs. There was a thunderous crack, and a ball of fire exploded above the branches. Debris went flying in every possible direction before the flames engulfed what remained of the tree.

Violet was too petrified to scream. Clinging to the open window, her eyes remained fixed while frightening thoughts ran through her mind. What if the horses were spooked by the lightning and the driver was unable to control them? They would run rampant until they pitched headlong into an open ravine or . . . .

Afraid to let her imagination go any further, Violet scrambled away from the door and huddled into a tight ball beneath her cloak. Finally, she felt the coach slowly drawing to a standstill. Feeling a bit foolish and even embarrassed by her seemingly unwarranted fears, she decided to feign sleep so she wouldn't have to look the driver in the face, or, worse yet, the handsome cowboy, who seemed all too eager to amuse himself by taking delight in her desperate plight.

The stagecoach stopped under what Violet assumed was some sort of a makeshift shelter. Besides her pounding heart, all she could hear were the horses jingling their harnesses and the heavy drumming of the rain. For an intense moment, she waited, wondering what the men were doing. The coach tipped awkwardly to one side then settled again before she sensed a presence near the window.

Chapter Two

"**S**he's asleep," the cowboy said in a quiet voice.

Violet watched through a crack she had formed near the edge of her cloak. The driver leaned heavily into the side of the coach. He dug tobacco from a worn-looking pouch and stuffed a shredded wad into his mouth. "Once this rain lets up, we can git back on the road," he responded. The driver paused for a moment. "This sure ain't no place for a lady the likes 0' her."

"Where do you suppose she's headed?" the cowboy asked, pushing his hat back, then propping his elbow inside the window before he turned sideways to face the driver.

"Jake, back at the hotel, said she was on the train to Wood River, same as you."

Violet quickly shut her eyes when the cowboy turned to peer into the dark compartment.

"Wonder if she's fixin' to take Sal's place at the school house."

"She don't look like no schoolmarm I ever seen," the driver said with a slow, dull drawl.

Violet stifled the urge to laugh. It didn't appear to her that either of them had ever seen the inside of a school house, much less a schoolmarm.

"You reckon she's a dance hall girl?" the driver wondered aloud.

Violet's desire to laugh suddenly turned to hostility. She clenched her fists and gritted her teeth to keep from screaming abuses at the good-for-nothing scoundrel.

"I don't know. Seems a bit too shy to me," the cowboy answered.

Violet thought for a moment, then decided being called shy at least was better than being called a dance hall girl.

It was quiet for what seemed a long time, except for the sound of the softening rain and the now distant rumble of thunder. Then the driver pushed away from the coach, squirted a stream of tobacco juice through the air, and said, "I heard about ol' Tippon. Did they catch the killer yet?"

The killer! Violet was stunned into disbelief. Her father was dead? The cowboy's reply vibrated in her head like the echoing clang of a bell.

"No, but we're pretty sure we know who's behind it all," the cowboy answered.

"Did he ever get any gold outta that ol' claim he'd been pannin' all these years?"

"Nothing a body'd brag on, but I reckon it kept him going, being out there all alone and all."

Tears filled Violet's eyes. It didn't have to be that way, she thought. She would have been happy growing up no matter where her father wanted to live, as long as he was there with her and her mother. She thought for a lingering moment about the life she had in St. Louis and realized there was no comparing it to what she'd been through in the past few days. Her mother had raised her to be a lady, like herself. It appeared her father had run off to become a gold miner. She had heard all about what gold could do to a man. In St. Louis, they called it gold fever. But there must have been more to it than just gold. That's what she was bound to find out.

*   *   *

As the storm receded, the stagecoach continued on its journey.

Violet had just finished brushing her hair and was about to pin it up when the door flew open and the cowboy slipped, boots first, into the coach.

Taking a moment to catch his breath, he said, "Excuse me, ma'am, but I figured you might be hungry since you didn't have time at Sander's Creek to pack a lunch."

Dropping her shoulders, Violet let out a repressed sigh. "Do you always come and go in such a haphazard manner?"

"Only when I see the need. Sorry if I woke you up."

Violet forced a smile. "I was already awake. But you're right about being hungry, if I wouldn't be imposing."

"It's no trouble. By the way, you got a name?"

Violet cringed. She was afraid he might ask her that, and she wasn't ready to hear about how her father had been killed. She dropped her eyelashes so she wouldn't have to see his reaction. "My name's Violet, Violet Tippon."

There was a brief moment of agonizing silence. "I was going to Wood River . . ." she paused, swallowing hard, "to see my father."

The cowboy promptly removed his hat. He lowered his eyes as he ran his long fingers through his black, wavy hair. "I sure am sorry, ma'am. I guess you heard what I told the driver, I mean about your pa. If I would've known I . . ."

Violet's eyes swelled with tears. "It wasn't your fault." A moment passed before she asked, "Did you know him?"

He nodded kindly. "Everyone knew Sam Tippon. I talked with him quite a few times myself. My name's Lance Tridel. I live at the Rough and Tumble Ranch. My aunt's the one who sent you the letter."

"He didn't have a stroke then, did he?" Violet asked.

Lance looked out the window, hesitating before he shook his head.

With her hand covering her lowered eyes, Violet gently bit her lip. It didn't appear that he was going to tell her any more, so there was no sense in asking. She laid her hand in her lap and looked at the cowboy's well-defined profile. His face was already sunburned, even though it was only the end of May.

Attempting to continue the conversation, she asked, "Do you think we'll make it to Wood River by tonight?"

Lance reached across the seat and pulled a strip of beef jerky from a leather pouch. He tore off a piece and handed it to Violet.

"The storm's held us up a bit," he said, "and we have a short stop at Bartlett. But if there's no more trouble, we'll pull in about sundown. The coach takes a lot longer than the train."

Wondering what he meant by trouble, Violet watched him as he bit a chunk out of the jerky and started chewing. She frowned before she bit into the piece he'd handed to her. It looked like shoe leather, but she was pleasantly surprised by its taste. It was not at all what she had expected, though it was a bit tough and sinewy.

"What is this?" she asked.

"Beef jerky," he replied. "It's pretty tasty with a hunk of this bread." He thrust out a handful of bread that he had tom from half a loaf wrapped in a checkered towel.

Violet smiled and took the bread and the piece of hard cheese he handed to her.

"Did you buy all of this food at Sander's Creek? Surely I owe you something."

Lance took a long gulp from a canteen then passed it to Violet. He shook his head. "A little gal over at the saloon made it for me. Didn't cost me a thing."

Violet's chin lifted slightly. Now that he knew she was Sam Tippon's daughter, surely he still didn't think she was one of those dance hall girls. She dropped her shoulders, suddenly not caring what he thought. She wasn't going to Texas to impress some old cowboy.

Lance and Violet finished their simple meal. Then Lance scooted down in the seat, stretching out his long legs just before he cast a sidelong glance in Violet's direction. He decided she was every bit as pretty as Sam had made out. With that thought in mind, he drew his wide-brimmed hat down over his eyes and within the next moment he was asleep.

Violet felt strange sitting in such close quarters with a sleeping cowboy. She made a mental note not to mention it to her mother and Aunt Tilly when she wrote home.

It was a long, boring drive. After a while, she grew tired of looking at the endless, dove-gray sky and the landscape that never seemed to change. She did like the way the wind smelled since it had rained, though. It was somehow different from the way it smelled back home. She thought she might like to embroider but decided against it. There wasn't enough light coming through the window. She remembered the telegram she had sent and wondered about her mother's reaction to it. She laid her head back and thought about her father and the kind of life he must have lived in Texas. Had he ever missed her or her mother? Did he ever really want to have children? Why did he leave? Now that she was in Texas, she wondered if it was too late to find answers to her questions.

Violet opened her eyes, only just then realizing that she had fallen asleep. She snapped open the cover on the watch pinned to her wide collar. It was close to five o'clock. Peering out the window, she was surprised to see some men on horseback riding a good distance from the road. She glanced at the sleeping figure across from her then back out the window.

There were three or four men riding toward the coach at a slow canter. After a moment, they stopped and leaned into their saddle horns. She began to worry.

"Mr. Tridel. Wake up." Violet nudged Lance's knee gently. "There's some men on horses. They appear to be following us."

Lance took in a deep breath and slid back in the seat. Pushing his hat back on his head, he looked bleary eyed. He yawned deeply before he leaned toward the window.

"They're horsemen, all right. Don't appear to be doin' any harm."

Violet's brow creased. "They aren't bandits, are they?" she asked.

"Bandits aren't usually so polite," Lance replied as he studied the riders.

"Polite?"

"They usually introduce themselves by pointin' a gun at ya'."

All expression left Violet's face. "When do you suppose we'll make it to Bartlett?" she asked in a weak voice.

"Ya' know what time it is?"

"About five o'clock."

"We ought to be pullin' in any time now."

Violet sighed. "I'll sure be glad when we get to Wood River."

Lance yawned again and stretched back into the seat until he filled half the coach. "So will I. I haven't been home for weeks. I'd like to sleep in my own bed for a change, and eat some of Aunt Ruth's cookin'."

Violet smiled. It seemed funny to hear such a tough—looking cowboy talk about getting back home. She glanced out the window, but there was no sign of the men on horseback. That was a relief. Maybe everything was going to be all right after all.

*   *   *

The stagecoach stopped in front of Bartlett Livery Stables. Lance opened the door and stepped into the dusty street. Then he turned to help Violet. The driver had leaped to the ground and was walking across the street when Lance led Violet toward the boardwalk.

"Soon as he picks up the mail and the horses are watered, we'll be leavin'," he said. "I'm headin' over to the sheriff's office to look at the 'wanted' posters."

Violet was about to ask him about the wanted posters when a tall, broad-shouldered man, dressed in shabby clothes and smelling strongly of horses, appeared carrying two buckets of water.

"Need any feed?" the man asked.

"No, water will be enough," Lance replied. "Last stop's Wood River."

The man plopped the buckets down in front of the lead horses then stood upright. He squared his shoulders and grinned broadly. "Well, this here must be the little lady we all been hearin' so much about. So, Tridel, when's the weddin'?"

Violet whirled around just in time to see Lance motioning for the liveryman to be quiet. "What wedding?" she retorted.

Unhindered by the stern expression on Lance's face, the liveryman's bellowing laugh filled the air. "Why, everyone in Texas is talkin' about it, ma'am. Heck, we ain't had a good weddin' since Fullerton's son got hitched up with that schoolmarm back in '85." He paused to consider. "Or maybe it was '87."

Having caught on to what "everyone in Texas was talking about," Violet thrust her shoulders back and tossed her head, her eyes flashing at Lance. "Why, you good-for-nothing cow-puncher! How dare you spread rumors like that about me."

Lance reared back when he thought he saw fire shooting out of Violet's eyes. "Now, hold on there, ma'am. You ain't heard the whole story yet."

"I've heard enough!" Violet stated firmly before she walloped him across the jaw with her bag, spun around, and marched across the street.

Lance rubbed the side of his face. "Now, look what you've gone and done, Cliff."

A puzzled look settled over the liveryman's face as he rubbed his whiskered jaw. "Huh. Leave it to a woman to go an' change her mind and not tell ya'."

"Oh, shut up," Lance growled, as he stormed off toward the jail.

"Don't you worry none. Soon as it gits dark, she'll come a runnin' back," the liveryman shouted after him.

Violet was never so angry in all her life. Her heart was racing a mile a minute while her eyes burned with tears of humiliation. She could barely see where she was headed. The sound of her heels pounding the boardwalk was her only assurance that she was still capable of comprehension. Elongated shadows cast by the sun setting behind the store-fronts indicated that night was close. Undaunted, however, she marched on, convincing herself that she didn't have to ride the rest of the way to Wood River with that lying, sneaking, good-for-nothing cowboy.

She stepped off the boardwalk and into the street that separated two buildings. Without warning, a giant figure lunged out and grabbed her, throwing her into the dark space between the buildings. Terror surged through her. An inner voice told her not to panic, but a swell of hysteria, like a mountainous wave, kept growing inside of her. Finally, almost without knowing it, she screamed as loud and as long as she could.

The man, whose face was covered by a scarf, towered over her, forming an ominous shadow. He covered her with a coarse, scratchy bag. The hem of her skirt was caught and she heard it rip just before he shoved her inside the bag and hauled her away, her body rolled up into an unbearable knot.

She tried to cry out, but there was barely room enough to breathe. Before she had time to consider what was happening, she felt herself being pulled up in front of someone on horseback.

As the horse sped away, she was jostled about until she felt light-headed and nauseous. It was worse than a nightmare. The air inside the gunnysack was gritty and stale, and any effort to catch her breath only made her head swim.

After a time, the horse skidded to a halt. The man swung the bag around, dropped it on the rocky ground, then dismounted. Violet cringed as pain shot through her body. All at once the man pulled open the bag and a burst of fresh air rushed in. Violet gasped and attempted to free herself, but a strong pair of gloved hands held her back.

"You ain't goin' nowhere, little lady. And just in case you're wonderin' who sent the welcomin' committee, it was a reputable man who don't take kindly to folks claimin' to own what rightfully belongs to him. Ya' just keep that in mind in case ya' decide to stick around a while."

With his open hand, the man shoved her back inside the bag and slipped a piece of rope loosely around the top. The next thing Violet heard was the sound of his horse pounding a fast retreat.

A painful throbbing grew inside Violet's head, and blood began trickling down the side of her face. She struggled in an attempt to release the tie on the bag, but found instead that the noose only seemed to tighten with each move she made.

As the moments ticked by, she felt herself growing weaker and realized there was no way she could free herself. The wind picked up, and cold shivers began to slither down her spine. She tried to think of anything but the intense darkness surrounding her. Periodic spasms of terror ricocheted through her body, magnifying her fear of what might linger outside the gunny sack. She fought to calm herself by repeating that the worst was over and she was still alive. For how long, though? That fear was impossible to squelch.

Then a new fear gripped her. Would she ever see her mother again? How long would she be able to breathe in the tightly woven bag? It was already so hard to breathe . . .

Her thoughts were cut off by a dark swimming sensation that quickly engulfed her.

*   *   *

By the time Lance heard the scream and came running out of the jail, the street was filled with a confusing mass of mumbling people. He hastily scanned the boardwalk and saw that Violet was nowhere in sight. Apprehension swelled inside him, and his face broke out in a cold, tingling sweat. Ol' Tippon always said he'd like to see Lance married to his daughter, but Lance had only been joking when he bragged about marrying her as soon as she got to town. If anything happened to her, he'd never be able to live with himself.

He quickly made his way through the crowd, inquiring hastily of anyone who seemed to know what had happened. Someone had seen a woman walking quickly down the boardwalk. There was a scream, and then she was gone.

Lance broke through the crowd and waved to the driver of the stagecoach, who had just come out of the general store. Lance told him that Miss Tippon had somehow disappeared and that he was to go on to Wood River. Lance would catch up as soon as he found her. Without waiting for a reply, he turned and ran to the livery where he ordered the liveryman to saddle up a fast horse. There was no time to waste. It was getting dark.

After a few anxious minutes, Lance leapt into the saddle, grabbed the reins, and swung the horse around, spurring him in the direction he had last seen Violet headed. Recalling how long he had heard the sound of her heels on the boardwalk, he figured that she had made it past the barbershop. He reined in near the hitching post closest to the building and dismounted. In the failing light, it was hard to see anything that might give him a clue, until he paused at the end of the boardwalk and bent his head to contemplate his next move. In the dirt at his feet, there were signs of a scuffle. He recognized a scrap of material and picked it up. Straining his eyes, he followed the trail of brushed dirt until he saw a man's boot imprints beside those of a horse. He whirled around, feeling the adrenaline rush through his body as he ran to his horse.

He'd been to Bartlett enough times to know there was a seldom-used road that led out of town toward the old mining camps. The road was also used by anyone who wanted to get out of town fast. Mounting in a wide swoop, he whipped his horse into a swift gait.

He wondered who would want to kidnap Violet Tippon, and why. She seemed harmless enough. It was all his fault. He should have watched out for her better, since she was traveling alone. If anyone laid a finger on ol' Tippon's daughter, he could bet he'd have the dickens to pay when he got back to the Rough and Tumble.

As the sky grew darker, Lance slowed his horse to a steady walk. It would be hard to see anything along the roadside if he was going too fast. Besides, if the culprits were hiding in the trees up ahead, they would be able to hear him coming at a faster pace. Half an hour went by before he noticed the stars coming out and a pale moon slowly rising. Soon it would be too dark to see anyone.

The thought of heading back to town and starting the search again in the morning had just occurred to him when he thought he saw something on the road up ahead. It was probably just a fallen branch, but he decided he'd better be sure. He nudged the horse on, and then drew his gun before he dismounted. He pulled back the hammer and cautiously made his way toward whatever was moving inside a bound gunnysack.

Violet was barely able to make out the sound of the approaching footsteps. Her mind wavered between a conscious and a semi-conscious state. Too weak to cry out for help, she managed a groan and a few feeble attempts to roll over inside the cramped space. Not knowing whose footsteps she heard, she hoped whoever was approaching would save her from what seemed to be certain death. Her only prayer was that the person was not the same man who had kidnapped her. Worse yet, she hoped there weren't any wild animals around.

After a few swift tugs on the rope, the bag fell open and Violet tumbled out in a crumpled heap, gasping for air. A man was huddled over her, asking a lot of rapid questions, but she was barely able to discern the meaning of his words. Nonetheless, she recognized, by the sound of his drawling voice, that it was Lance Tridel.

"You're ok, ma'am. Everything's gonna to be all right."

Violet mumbled some unintelligible words as she was being lifted carefully off the ground; then a swirling whirlpool filled her head just before she fainted.

Lance's heart pounded in his head as he mounted his horse, cradling the woman next to his chest. He contemplated what to do for a moment before spurring the gelding into a swaying gallop. He wasn't sure how long Violet had been tied up in that bag, but she had lost a lot of blood. He needed to find a doctor—and fast. He knew there wasn't a doctor in Bartlett, so his only choice was to ride at breakneck speed to Wood River. It was risky with her lying limp in his arms and weak as a kitten, but it was a chance he would have to take.

It was a long, exhausting ride, but Lance made it to the Rough and Tumble close to midnight. At the sound of his fast approach, a couple of ranch hands came running out of the bunkhouse, climbing into their pants, shirttails flapping in the wind. At about the same time, the front screen door flew open, and Lance's uncle came running out half dressed. His aunt, clinging to her wrapper, followed close on his heels. Lance handed Violet down to one of the hands who quickly followed his aunt back into the house. In a bone tired voice, Lance ordered one of the men to ride out for the doctor. Then he nearly fell out of the saddle. In a minute, his uncle was at his side.

"Bill told us to be watchin' out for ya'. Where'd ya' find the girl?"

With his head hanging wearily, his shoulders sagging, Lance dragged himself over to the water pump and took off his hat. He pumped just enough water to splash on his face. "On Dicey Road, just outside of Bartlett. She was tied up in a gunnysack."

Ben Tridel groaned. "Ya' have any idea who done it?"

Lance looked straight ahead at the lighted windows of the house, his knitted brows fixed, his lips pressed firmly together. A moment passed. He slapped his hat against his thigh, shook his head, and started toward the house. There was nothing they could do now but wait.

Chapter Three

When Violet opened her eyes, the room swayed, so she quickly closed them again. She felt sharp pain in her head, and the slightest movement made her all too aware of her aching muscles. The floor squeaked. Through heavy lashes, she strained to see a blurred outline of a woman.

"Well, we were beginnin' to wonder if you was ever gonna come around."

Violet winced in pain. "Who . . . Who are you?"

"My name's Ruth Tridel," the woman at Violet's bedside explained. "My husband, Ben, owns the Rough 'n' Tumble Ranch, where you're at now."

She bent down and smoothed the quilt on Violet's bed. Then, standing straight up with her hands on her wide hips, Ruth continued. "You lost a lot of blood layin' out on Dicey Road so long. We thought we was gonna lose you for sure."

Slowly, the past events unfolded in Violet's mind. "How long have I been here?"

"Four days," Ruth answered.

"How . . ."

"My nephew, Lance, brought you here. He said you were on the stagecoach and then when . . . well, when things went wrong, he brought you here."

Violet moaned.

"Now don't you worry none, Miss Tippon. We were good friends of your pa's, and we mean to take care of you till you decide what to do about . . ."

"I've already decided what to do," Violet interrupted. "My mother was right. This country's no place for me, and I mean to go back to St. Louis as soon as the next stagecoach comes through."

"Well, that'd be tomorrow, but anyone can see you're in no condition to git on the stage."

Violet weakly brushed a tear from her cheek. "Well, I can't stay here. It just wouldn't be right."

"Why not?"

"I can't just lie here and let strangers take care of me."

The woman's face softened. "It's not like we were strangers, honey. Your pa was like family."

Violet turned her face into the white pillow slip that smelled of brisk air and sunshine. She knew the woman's kind words were meant to console her, but instead they had saddened her. It was hard to face the fact that these strangers were helping her because they knew her father better than she did.

The amply built woman turned and walked toward a small, makeshift dressing table. Someone had set up two empty crates, placed a board over them, and then tacked a piece of calico around the sides so that the table appeared less crude. The room, though simple, was clean and filled with the scent of wildflowers.

"I hope you don't mind that I put your things out for you. I thought it might make you feel more at home when you woke up and saw them."

"Thank you," Violet said. "But you shouldn't have gone to so much trouble."

"It was no trouble a'tall." The woman turned around. A perplexed look crossed her face as she examined a strange—looking piece of iron. "As a matter of fact, it's been a might interestin' seein' all the doodads you brought with ya'."

Violet laughed weakly. "That's a crimping iron. I curl my hair with it. When I feel better, I'll do yours, if you'd like."

Ruth quickly laid the crimping iron on the table. "I'm not much for primpin'. Never had the time, or the need for such." She lightly touched a neatly arranged row of ear bobs and a pearl-handled brush before she slowly picked up the matching mirror. She hesitantly looked at herself before setting it down. Then she picked up something that resembled a lamb's tail. "What's this?" Ruth asked in a curious, childlike voice.

"That's a powder puff for putting on dusting powder," Violet said. "You put it on after a bath."

"Of all things!" Ruth chuckled, as she carefully dabbed the puff on her open palm. "Your pa would'a sure been proud."

"Did he say anything before he died? Did he ask about me?" Violet questioned in a gentle voice.

"He asked us to bury him on Tangleweed, and he left something here for you."

Ruth set the puff down on the table and walked over to a worn armoire across the room. Violet wondered at the woman as she rummaged through it. She had on a plain dress made of navy blue broadcloth, and a printed apron. Her sleeves were rolled back to the elbow and her forearms were tanned and firm. Her brown hair, which was just beginning to show signs of gray, was knotted in back with short wisps circling her face. Violet was beginning to wonder what the woman was searching for when Ruth turned around.

"I know it's in here somewhere. It'd no doubt answer all your questions. But if you're gonna give up so quick and head back to St. Louis, I have a notion to change my mind. You wouldn't really need it then. It would only be a story to you there."

Violet wondered what this stranger could possibly have that she would need. "What is it?" she asked.

Ruth came toward the bed, her arms crossed over her rounded bosom. "Your pa told me if anything ever happened to him I was to give you this here book." She slipped the book out of the folds of her apron. "He told me where to find you if he . . ."

"Then he was killed," Violet said, more to herself than to the woman standing beside her.

Ruth's mouth curled up on the side. "What ever gave you that notion?"

"I overheard your nephew and the stagecoach driver talking about it."

"Yeah, I can imagine those two jawin' it up."

"Your nephew meant no harm, Mrs. Tridel. A storm came up, and the driver pulled the stagecoach off the road. They thought I was asleep when really I was . . . well, I was afraid of the lightning."

Ruth's laugh shook her entire body. "I ain't never heard of anyone bein' afraid of a rainstorm before. Guess it takes all kinds."

Violet didn't like being made fun of, but that seemed trivial compared to all that had happened since she left home. When she realized that Mrs. Tridel was staring at her, Violet wondered when she had last had another woman to talk to. In a tired voice, she said, "You wrote in your letter that my father had a stroke."

Ruth turned her head to one side and lowered her eyes. "I didn't have the heart to tell ya' he was killed. We could hardly believe it ourselves. Besides, your pa told me to write that in the letter just before he died."

Shocked, Violet tried to sit up until Ruth stopped her by gently pushing her back onto the propped pillows. "But why?" Violet pleaded. "Did he know that someone wanted to kill him?"

Ruth sat on the edge of the bed before she handed Violet the black leather bound book. "I don't know what to tell ya', honey. Maybe you'll find the answers in here. If you'd at least stay until we can make some sense of what's been goin' on . . . well, we'd be much obliged to ya'."

Violet took the book and opened it, slowly turning the first few pages. "It's a journal," she breathed, her heart beating quickly. Tears were on her lashes, and Ruth quickly dried them with the hem of her apron.

"Now I've gone and upset ya'."

Violet reached for Ruth's arm, and she shook her head. Hesitant at first, she looked up into the woman's kindly face. "It isn't that," she said. "It's just that this is all I have left of my father. You don't know what that means to me. Maybe now . . ." She paused. "There's so many unanswered questions, so many empty years."

"I was only s'pose to give that book to ya' if you agreed to come to Wood River. Somehow your pa would know then that you cared. You don't appear to me to be no quitter, but you still haven't said you'd stay."

Violet smiled. "I'11 only stay if you'll give me something to do to repay you for all your kindness."

Ruth patted Violet's hand. "It wasn't kindness, honey. Ol' Tippon talked about you so much I feel like you're part of the family. Kinda like the little girl I never had." This time there were tears in Ruth's eyes. She stood up and smoothed out her apron. "Now we went and talked so much I'm afraid you got yourself all tired out. The doctor'll have my hide for that."

Violet couldn't help but grin. "I won't tell, if you won't."

"Now you're talkin' sense," Ruth said, as she started toward the door. She opened it slowly and then stopped to look over her shoulder. "Git some rest now. There's a fella who's been mighty worried about you. He won't believe you're better if he sees you as pale as you are now and movin' as weak as a newborn kitten."

Ruth shut the door softly behind her as Violet's face flushed a deep pink.

∗   ∗   ∗

Another few days passed before Violet was strong enough to dress herself and cross the room all in one day without feeling faint. Still, her legs wobbled as she managed her way to the kitchen. It was Monday morning, and the men had left for the south pasture where they were rounding up cattle for branding. When she came through the door, Ruth turned around, surprised to see that Violet was wearing a blue poplin dress instead of her wrapper.

"Well, if you ain't a busy one today. I suppose you're gonna want to knead this here bread dough before you start on the noon fixin's."

Violet smiled. "I might be able to set the plates on the table, but to tell you the truth, I've never made bread before . . . or fixin's either, whatever they are."

Ruth chuckled, her floured hands slapping together. "We'll see to that when the time comes. Right now, you just go ahead and sit down and I'll get you a glass of milk and some muffins I made fresh this mornin'. How about a couple of eggs and some good home-cured bacon?"

Violet shook her head as she drew a chair out from under the table and sat down. "Milk and muffins will be plenty. Thank you, Mrs. Tridel."

Ruth's smile covered her entire face. "If you keep on sayin' 'thank you' for everything I do and say, and go on callin' me Miz Tridel every time you look at me, you'll get plumb worn out just talkin'. Folks 'round here save all that fancy talk for weddin's and funerals and such."

Without waiting for a reply, she busied herself with getting breakfast. Violet looked around the crude ranch house, allowing a feeling of warmth to grow inside her. Everything was so different here. The walls were in sore need of paint, and the furnishings were plain. The windows were decorated with simple muslin curtains. Despite what seemed to be lacking, there was a feeling of belonging and hominess.

Back in St. Louis, Violet's family had a maid who was quite prim and proper and suitably dressed. She never spoke unless she was spoken to. Violet's mother and Aunt Tilly were always fashionably attired, their hair done up in the latest style, whether they went out or not. Violet tried to imagine her mother wearing an apron, but her thoughts were interrupted by the sound of Ruth's hearty voice.

"The men'll be comin' in 'round noon to eat. It'd be nice if you could sit up at the table with us." Ruth set a plate down in front of Violet.

"Well . . ."

"I know it'd sure put Lance's mind at ease if he was to see you up and around a bit. He sure felt bad about not keepin' a better eye out for you."

A puzzled look formed on Violet's brow. "Why? It wasn't his fault at all. I insisted on leaving St. Louis, knowing full well there might be danger."

Ruth's mouth turned down and she wagged her head from side to side in a matter-of-fact sort of way. "He's always been an obligin' sorta fella," she said. "I guess he figured it was what your pa would have expected of him. By the way, if you don't mind my askin', don't ladies like yourself usually travel with some sorta companion?"

Violet's hands came together at her waist as she quickly looked away. "I did have a companion. Hattie was quite elderly. She . . . she died at a hotel the first night after we left St. Louis."

Ruth shook her head. "You poor thing. You sure have had a time of it."

Violet ate a muffin, waiting to mention that she had started reading her father's diary. She wanted to absorb what she could before she allowed any further input. Still, she was curious enough to listen to anything these people had to offer.

"Does anyone have any idea who might have killed my father and why? Or why someone would have wanted to scare me away?"

Ruth turned slowly, her hands flat against her apron. "We all got our ideas, honey, but no proof; so I won't be namin' any names. Ben and Lance were hopin' you'd feel up to talkin' some about what happened in Bartlett. Maybe it'd give 'em some clue as to what happened to your pa."

Violet turned her head to the side, her lips closed tightly. After a moment she said, "I would like to settle matters as soon as possible, and then leave for home. If no one knows who killed my father, then surely there's nothing I can do about it."

"Don't ya' wanna know why your pa was killed?"

A look of uncertainty spread over Violet's face. "Whoever killed my father must be the same person who tried to scare me. Maybe he was hoping I wouldn't stay in Texas."

"You mean to let him have his way?" Ruth asked, her voice stern.

Violet dropped her shoulders with a quick sigh. "When I left St. Louis, I thought my father was alive. I had so many unanswered questions. Now he's gone, and there's nothing I can do, but keep myself from being killed, too." She paused to take a drink. "Besides, my mother's very sick, and I promised to return as soon as things were settled here."

"You'll still talk to Ben, won't ya'?" Ruth wondered aloud.

Violet nodded as she rose to her feet. "I'd like to rest a while before they come in."

"You do look a bit green," Ruth said in a low voice, thinking how frail city girls were. "I'll knock on your door a little before noon. Give ya' a chance to spruce up some."

"Thank you Miz, I mean Ruth," Violet said. Holding onto the railing, she climbed the stairs to her room. She closed the door then went to the bed where she sat down. She picked up the diary that she had left on the table next to the bed and looked hard at the cover. Her eyes clouded with uncertainty. Maybe the real reason she wanted to go back to St. Louis was because she was afraid. Since she had been reading her father's diary, there was no doubt left in her mind that someone had killed him in order to claim Tangleweed. But why? From what little she had seen of Wood River, she doubted that anyone would kill for the land, unless they wanted it to graze cattle on. There was only one way to find out. As soon as she felt stronger, she would have to go see Tangleweed for herself.

* * *

A light knock on the door was followed by the sound of fading footsteps. Violet opened her eyes, only then realizing that she had fallen asleep. She must have needed the rest, for she found she felt better when she got up and began to move about. The smell of meat frying and bread baking floated up from the kitchen. It felt good to wake up to such sweet, warm aromas. She smoothed the wrinkles from her dress and touched up her hair before she started downstairs.

The kitchen was full of rough-looking men, all eager to eat, all talking loudly at once. When Violet walked into the room, the men abruptly stopped what they were doing. Their voices dropped to a low murmur while they stared at her.

"Well, don't stand there gawkin' like a bunch'a barn owls," Ruth barked. "You'll make the poor thing wish she'd never set foot on the place."

It seemed all the men turned their heads away at the same time, each one bustling to find his place at the long table. The quick shuffling of boots, chairs scraping across the wood floor, the clatter of plates, and the clanking of flatware filled the room. Someone asked for the potatoes; another asked for the platter of meat. Before Violet realized it, everyone's plate was filled, and the robust men were eating heartily. Ruth bustled up to the table and started slicing the bread.

"Come sit over here." She motioned to Violet with a slight toss of her head.

As Violet moved toward her seat, one of the men sprang up out of his chair, whipped off his dusty shapeless hat, and seated her with as much grace as Violet figured a tall, gangly cowboy could manage. The room grew quiet. Everyone seemed to stop dead in their tracks.

"Thank you," she said timidly, hoping no one noticed how nervous she was. All eyes remained fixed on her. It seemed as if the men were waiting for her to make the next move. Violet picked up her fork. She wondered if, perhaps at some point in their lives, they had been exposed to some form of etiquette.

"What's that crawlin' on your plate, Roscoe?" Ben called out, his voice breaking through the heavy silence. Aghast, Violet dropped her fork. Her eyes opened wide as she gasped. Loud, boisterous laughter filled the room.

Lance, who was seated across from Violet, shouted above the noise, "Nothin' to be alarmed about, ma'am. That's just Uncle Ben's way of lettin' the boys know time's a wastin'."

The color slowly came back to Violet's face, but her appetite was gone. A subtle rumble vibrated over the table as platters of food were passed around for anyone who was ready for seconds. Violet seemed to be forgotten in the bustle, of which she was relieved. She breathed easier, concluding that one thing was for certain: This meal, if it could be called that, could in no way be compared to one of her mother's dinner parties, or her Aunt Tilly's elegant teas.

Violet considered it a good thing she didn't have to confront this sort of ruckus every day. Soon she would be heading back to St. Louis.

"You look a lot better than the last time I saw ya'."

Violet looked straight into Lance's gray eyes. Without thinking, she touched a faded bruise near her cheek while smiling at his gentle concern. Lance returned her gaze, until she began to feel uncomfortable. She cleared her throat and cast a quick, wary glance at the scraggly faces turned in her direction. For the first time since her "coming out" party when she was 16, she was at a loss for words, not knowing how to make a reply to a room full of inquisitive men. All she could think to say was, "Thank you."

Ben coughed then made a gravelly sound when he cleared his throat. It seemed to serve its purpose. The men looked at him then started eating like nothing had happened. Though hesitant at first, Violet looked toward the end of the table, wondering what kind of a look or sign Ben had flashed at the men.

Without leaving so much as a clue, Ben wiped his white-whiskered face with his open palm and reached for his coffee cup. "As I was headin' out this mornin', just after you boys left, Doss, from over at Thurman's place, rode up with word that Thurman's boy Joey died last night."

Ruth stopped what she was doing and shook her head. "Poor thing. He had the croup pretty bad," she said in a low voice. "First his wife, now one of his boys. I wonder if that man's ever gonna see the back side of trouble."

"Maybe you and Miss Tippon oughta ride over there this afternoon with some fixin's," Ben added.

Ruth quickly glanced at Violet. "If Violet feels up to it."

Violet gently set down her glass of water and nodded in agreement, glad to finally be able to do something besides sleep all day. "I would be more than happy to go," she said eagerly.

Just then, several men got up to leave, the sound of clomping boots filling the room as they headed for the door. The remaining three cowboys, loudly chewing their food, suddenly slammed their palms on the table, shoved back their chairs, and donned their hats, one of them tugging on his shapeless vest as they headed for the door. They all thanked Ruth, who had just sat down to eat, then, in turn, crammed on their hats then tipped their twisted hat brims to Violet. Violet noticed that Ruth's face was one big, proud smile as she watched the men grab what remained of the biscuits just before they tumbled out onto the sunlit porch. One man couldn't keep from belching just before he stuffed the side of mouth full of chewing tobacco. The door slammed shut on the silhouetted forms before there was a scrambling sound followed by the pounding of horses' hooves.

Violet, whose stomach was turning queasy, felt somewhat awkward and confused. Surely her mother would have fainted dead away if she knew what sort of company Violet was keeping. On the other hand, Violet was touched by the mens' simple attempts to gain her acceptance and approval. There was no doubt in her mind why the place was called Rough and Tumble, or any question that, for the rest of her time there, the daily meals were going to take some getting used to.

"I been meanin' to ask ya', Miss Tippon," Ben's resonant voice interrupted Violet's thoughts. "By any chance did ya' git a look at the fella who nabbed ya' when ya' got off the stage in Bartlett?"

Violet took a deep breath, her narrow shoulders squared as she folded a frayed napkin in her lap. She looked at Ruth, who smiled kindly at her, and then at Lance, who was looking down at the fork he was twisting between his fingers. It was hard for her to believe that only a moment ago, he seemed so worried about her. Now it appeared his thoughts were elsewhere. He was probably thinking how childish she had been for running away from him in Bartlett in the first place. She pursed her lips to stifle an angry groan when she recalled the reason for running away, and then looked straight at Ben.

"No, sir." She paused. "All I remember was him saying something like, 'If you're wondering who sent the welcoming committee, it was a reputable . . . '"

Lance's head shot up and Violet started. After a terse moment she swallowed back the pain of the vivid memory and went on.

"' . . . a reputable man who doesn't take kindly to folks claiming what rightfully belongs to him.'"

Violet nearly jumped out of her skin when lance sprang to his full, imposing height, his chair hitting the floor.

"Hold on there, son," Ben circled the table in two long strides and grabbed Lance's arm that was taut all the way down to his doubled fist. Lance's face was red, and his eyes were filled with a rage that shot flames of steel blue. Violet had never seen anyone so angry in all her life.

31

"That dirty low-down . . ."

"Lance!" Ruth cut off his accusation. "Don't go accusin' anyone till we got more proof."

"Or till someone else is dead," Lance growled, jerking his arm away from his uncle's firm grip. He threw a dark, sidelong glance at Violet then stormed out of the room, slamming the door so hard the whole house shook.

Trembling uncontrollably, Violet stared wide-eyed at Ben, who stood across the table from her. His lined brow hooded his dark eyes that nearly bore a hole through the door. "Dad-gum him and his temper. If he don't watch out, he'll be the one who gits hisself killed next."

Chapter Four

*U*sually Lance ain't one for sparrin'," Ruth said as soon as Ben slammed the door. "Mostly, he walks away from a fight." Crossing her arms over her ample bosom, she shook her head. "But that Ben___ he gets his dander up 'bout most anything these days."

When they heard Ben calling to Lance somewhere out in the yard, Ruth lifted the curtain and craned her neck until she could see Lance. She frowned sternly. Fearing a ruckus she dropped the curtain and huffed then started stacking plates.

"We got a minute since Lance is hitchin' up the team," she said to Violet. "If you want to finish clearin' the table, put the rest of the dishes in the dishpan and the leftover food on that table over there." She wagged her soapy hand toward a table across the room. "I'll start gettin' a few things together to take over to the Thurmans."

Violet had never cleared a table before, but she was too embarrassed to admit it. Afraid that she might drop and break something, she decided to carry only what she could in one hand. She walked back and forth, carrying one cup and then another, a handful of forks, and then a handful of knives. Violet's face glowed with pride in her accomplishment.

Ruth didn't have the heart to ask Violet what she was doing. She had heard that city folks had some peculiar ways. Maybe this was one of them. She was simply glad to have a woman around the place to talk to.

"I don't mean to pry," Violet said as she walked back to the table, "but I was wondering what happened to Mr. Thurman's wife."

Since Violet was still clearing the table, Ruth decided to scrape the frying pans. "A couple years back, after Claire had Abe, her youngest, she

33

got milk fever and died." Ruth stopped what she was doing and looked up, her eyes fixed on the wall across from her. "Worst case I ever saw."

Violet set a chipped coffee cup in the dishpan and turned around, her eyes full of concern. She vaguely recalled a conversation between her mother and some ladies who had come to tea one afternoon. One of the women had mentioned that one of her servants had had a baby and then died of milk fever.

"It must be a sad thing to be lying there dying, knowing you're leaving a baby behind." Violet looked at Ruth, her eyes filled with unspoken possibilities. "Who took care of the baby?"

"Lindsey, their oldest girl," Ruth replied.

"Did Mr. Thurman ever remarry?"

Ruth shook her head. "Nobody 'round these parts to marry." She paused, chortling softly. "That is, till you come along."

Violet whirled around, not realizing that the back door had just opened. "Why, I could never marry a cowboy," she blurted, just before Lance leaned over the threshold and grabbed the gloves he had left on the table. He grinned at Violet, looking straight into her eyes until her face started to blush like a budding rose.

"You ever eat crow, ma'am?" he said amiably.

Violet winced, her nose wrinkled in disgust. "Of course not!" she said without hesitating.

"Someday you'll find yourself likin' it real well," Lance said in a pleasant voice, before he tipped his hat brim and backed out the doorway.

Violet looked at Ruth who had a subdued grin on her face. "Whatever did he mean by that?" she asked.

Ruth shrugged. "Hard tellin'," she said just before she covered her mouth with her folded hand.

The door closed on Lance's laughter. Violet and Ruth watched him through the window as he swaggered across the yard, full of confidence, the tune he whistled filling the spring air.

It seemed a good time to leave. Ruth tied on her poke bonnet, and Violet put on a finely woven straw hat, which had a colorful band set off by a small cluster of flowers and a narrow cascade of ribbons. Ruth hoisted the basket of food into the wagon before she and Violet climbed up onto the spring seat and started down Green Acre Road toward the Thurmans.

*   *   *

Violet had nearly forgotten how exhilarating spring could be. Her attention was at once directed to the open countryside where the birds flitted amongst the budding trees, their songs rising above the clopping sound of the horse's hooves. Squirrels scurried to hide in the underbrush as the wagon passed by. Violet's head fell back and she gazed wide-eyed at the blue sky. "I never thought the country could be so beautiful," she mused.

Ruth breathed in the sweet fragrance of the wildflowers. "I reckon Texas kind of grows on a person. Before ya' know it, ya' been in one place all your life. But that don't seem to matter when it's a place like Wood River."

Surprised, Violet asked, "You mean you've never lived anywhere else?"

Ruth shifted the reins. "No. Like I said, it don't seem to matter. I grew up in these parts, and one day Ben come along lookin' for a place to put down his roots and, well, I kinda helped him make up his mind. In his younger days, Ben traveled all over the country. After we got married, we'd sit up late at night in front of the fire, and he'd tell me about all his adventures. So, in a way, I guess ya' could say I did my sight-seein' through him."

A feeling of warmth spread over Violet. She was beginning to like Ruth Tridel. She was drawn to the woman's kindly nature and her unselfish concern for everything and everyone around her. Violet had never felt so at ease with anyone before. She was so absorbed in her thoughts that Ruth's question went unnoticed. It wasn't until she felt Ruth's eyes on her that Violet came out of her daze.

"What did you say?"

Ruth's grin filled her entire face. "This country has that effect on people," she said. "I asked you what ya' did back in St. Louis. Folks been wonderin' if you're a schoolmarm."

Violet smiled, remembering Lance's conversation with the coach driver. "I'm a milliner," she replied. "I work in a seamstress shop designing hats to go with dresses that are special ordered."

Ruth peered at Violet's bonnet. "Did ya' make the one you're wearin'?"

Violet nodded. "Yes, as a matter of fact, I did."

Ruth looked back at the road then lightly snapped the reins. "Hmm, so that's what's in them fancy boxes. If that don't beat all. Too bad you ain't a schoolmarm, though. We don't need a mill . . . a hat maker, but we could sure use a schoolmarm."

A look of astonishment came over Violet's face. The way the Tridels assumed that she intended to stay in Wood River was perplexing to her. There seemed to be no question about her future; the Tridels had it all mapped out. Since she wasn't in the mood to challenge her future just yet, she decided it would be best to change the subject.

"My father wrote in his diary that he 'netted' Tangleweed in a card game. Mother never said anything about him being a gambler."

"Seems like gamblin' and gold diggin' kinda go hand in hand. But then I reckon there's lots about your pa ya' don't know. That's why he wanted ya' to have the diary. As for how he got Tangleweed, well, you'll have to talk to Ben about that. He was there that night."

Violet hesitated, afraid to say what she was thinking. Her mother never had a kind word to say about men who wasted their time or money. Maybe her father's gambling had caused them to have disagreements which had then caused their separation. Violet sighed heavily, frustrated at her inability to discern the past. Nonetheless, she had to know if her father had been an honest man.

"He played fair, didn't he?" she asked quick and to the point.

"If you're thinkin' your pa was killed cause he was a cheat you can put your mind to rest. Your pa was a descent man in any man's book. More than likely the fella sittin' across from him was the cheat."

Relieved, Violet settled back against the seat. Everyday her father was becoming more a part of her life instead of a man in a faded photograph.

As they came over a rise in the road, Ruth gently pulled on the reins to slow the horses. Violet saw a simple farm house with a rail fence around the yard. As they drew nearer, she could see the house needed paint, but the curtains, fluttering in the open windows, made it seem homey. There were a few apple trees in bloom, and one of them had a rope swing tied to a spanning bough. Near the side of the house there was a lilac bush, and just beyond that, Violet saw a clothesline with some sheets whipping about a forked branch that held the sagging line up. As they turned into the curved drive, a young girl appeared from the side of the house, carrying a clothes basket on her hip.

"That's Lindsey," Ruth said, waving at the girl.

The girl waved back but didn't smile.

Violet felt a twinge of pain in her heart, a feeling she'd never felt toward a stranger. When Lindsey approached the wagon, Violet realized how young she was. She thought that Lindsey couldn't be over 16. She had soft, brown eyes with long lashes and hair the color of honey.

"Lindsey, this is Violet Tippon. She's ol' man Tippon's daughter. She'll be stayin' with us for awhile—at least till she settles things over at Tangleweed." There was a brief pause while both girls nodded their greetings, Lindsey keeping her eyes lowered.

"We was real sorry to hear about Joey," Ruth added consolingly. "We brought over a few things we thought you might be needin'."

Lindsey shuffled her feet uneasily and turned her head to one side. "Thank you, Miz Tridel."

Violet felt a lump in her throat that was hard to swallow. "Is there anything else we can do to help?" she asked.

Without looking up, Lindsey shook her head. "Pa don't wanta see anyone just now."

Violet climbed down from the wagon. Ruth groaned as she bent over and lowered the basket she had prepared into Violet's ready hands. Violet walked up to Lindsey and set the basket on the ground before she placed a caring hand on the girl's shoulder.

When Lindsey's tears spattered the checkered cloth covering the basket, Violet turned her head toward the sound of the wind, her lips pressed firmly together. "Perhaps another day we can come by and help," she said. "For now, I think it would be best if you would wear this."

Violet reached up, took off her hat, and placed it carefully on Lindsey's head. "My mother always said working in the hot sun can wear you out if you don't keep your head covered."

Lindsey set down her clothes basket, her fingers shaking as they touched the rim of the finely woven straw hat. "That's mighty kind of you, Miss Tippon, but I'm sure this ain't no work bonnet."

"Use it for whatever you like, Lindsey," Violet said in a kind voice. "It's yours now."

The girl's head shot up. "Why, I could never keep anything as pretty as this," she cried.

"I have others." Violet paused. "I made it myself, in St. Louis where I work in a milliner's shop." She reached out and touched Lindsey's hand.

"It would mean a great deal to me if you would accept it as a gift," she added.

Before Lindsey could offer a reply, a man on horseback came galloping into the yard.

*   *   *

"Whoa," the man shouted in a strong, commanding voice, pulling hard on the reins before swiftly dismounting.

Violet noticed at once that he was tall and broad-shouldered. He wore fine clothes like those of a gentleman, something she had seen little of since she left home. When he removed his hat to greet them, Violet noticed his light brown hair was combed back with a soft crop of curls at the nape of his neck. His hazel eyes narrowed beneath brows that lined his prominent forehead. But his jaw, jutting slightly to the left, was his most striking feature, giving him an air of respectability and dignity. Violet was just wondering where he had come from when he turned toward her, his hat cradled in his hand, and nodded in greeting.

"You must be Miss Tippon. I'm Ralph Nolan, and I must say, I'm more than pleased to meet you, ma'am." His voice was unusually deep, his words well chosen and precise, uncommon to what Violet had come to expect from anyone living in Wood River.

She inclined her head briefly. "Thank you. It's a pleasure meeting you, too."

"It appears that you've met with some sort of accident, Miss Tippon," he said, as he carefully studied the paling bruises on Violet's face.

Violet had forgotten that, without the protective rim of her hat, the bruises would show. She was afraid she didn't look the part of the respectable lady she had been brought up to be. After hesitating, she touched her face lightly. "Well, yes, I did meet with a slight accident, Mr. Nolan. But I'm fine now."

Ralph Nolan smiled pleasantly. "You'll be pleased to know the whole town's been talking about you and your claim to Tangleweed."

"I don't know that that would please me, Mr. Nolan."

The man looked at her with what appeared to be well trained, admiring eyes. "Oh, but everything they've said about you is true. It is, indeed, a rarity in these parts to meet such a charming, young lady as yourself. Any effort I made to ride out here this afternoon was worth my time."

"I was under the impression, Mr. Nolan, that you came to see the Thurmans," Violet retorted.

Nolan laughed and glanced toward Lindsey, who had taken off her hat to admire it and was now shading her eyes from the sun with the back of her hand. "And you were absolutely right, Miss Tippon. But your being here has made it a pleasant task."

Ruth, who had remained seated in the wagon, rolled her eyes and cleared her throat several times. "Looks like we'd better be headin' back," she said, loud enough to be heard above Nolan's flattery.

"Please allow me to help you into the wagon," Nolan said, offering Violet his arm.

Violet slipped her arm through Nolan's before she turned to say good-bye to Lindsey, who timidly thanked her for the bonnet. Nolan smiled at Violet as he led her to the wagon. He then grasped her waist with his hands and lifted her in a quick, delicate swoop into the seat beside Ruth.

Violet felt her face flush and hoped Mr. Nolan would think it was the heat affecting her and not his unusually kind manner.

"Miss Tippon, have you been out to your father's claim yet?"

"Why, no, I haven't," Violet said plainly. "As a matter of fact, I was thinking about seeing if I could go tomorrow."

"Then by all means, won't you allow me to escort you?"

Violet looked at Ruth, who had a distrustful look in her eye, then back at Nolan. "Well, I . . ."

"The Tridels are pretty busy folks, but as for me, well, I have tomorrow to myself. I would be more than pleased to spend it in service to a fine, young lady such as yourself."

Violet was afraid to look at Ruth. The woman's sighs were enough to tell her that she had had enough of Nolan. Instead, with her eyes averted, she smiled and said, "That would be fine, Mr. Nolan. Good day."

Ruth snapped the reins and the horse started off down the road with Nolan's voice trailing after them.

"Good-bye, Miss Tippon, Mrs. Tridel. See you in the morning."

"'See you in the mornin'.' I don't like it," Ruth mimicked in disgust, "and I won't feel like myself till I put some distance between me and that insufferable laggard."

"He seemed kind enough," Violet said, disappointed by Ruth's bluntness.

Ruth turned her head and looked at Violet, her face wrinkled in disbelief. "Ya' don't mean to tell me ya' fell for all that gibberish." She snapped the reins so sharply the harness rattled as the horse picked up speed. "Folks ain't always what they seem to be. If ya' want my opinion, any woman who'd fall for a man with that snake-in-the-grass look in his eye has got a lot of learnin' to do."

Violet pursed her lips, her brow gathering in a frown. She turned her head toward the road, no longer mesmerized by the beauty of spring or hypnotized by the scent of wildflowers. The sun glittering through the treetops meant nothing to her as the countryside passed in a blur while a flood of mixed emotions assailed her, the least of them being the manner in which Ralph Nolan had conducted himself. Ruth was plainly disappointed in her for accepting his invitation. She sighed. Maybe she had been a bit hasty, but she was eager to see her father's claim and the place where he had lived all those years while she was growing up.

Looking around, Violet could see there weren't a lot of tall trees in Texas, like she was used to, just open country that went on for miles. She noticed a few clouds gathering on the horizon, which led her to think about rain and the sound of the unrelenting wind until her imagination drew a vivid picture of Texas in the dead of winter. Suddenly she felt all alone. She wondered if it was possible for a person to die of loneliness. She recalled the grief in Lindsey's eyes. She looked down at her frilled, pink nainsook dress; fingered the burgundy sash; and couldn't help but remember Lindsey's worn, brown skirt and blouse made of faded broadcloth.

She tried to tell herself that Lindsey was used to the life she lived, but it wasn't working. Lindsey was too young to be caring for a family. Surely she desired pretty dresses and parties and a gentleman caller. She wondered if anyone called on her. Surely Lance had noticed her.

"Does Lindsey have any gentleman callers?" she asked.

"You mean a beau?"

Violet nodded.

"Well, I know she was fixin' to marry Jed Turner before her ma died."

"And now they're not getting married?"

Ruth stared straight ahead, cradling the reins in her callused hand. "Why, who'd take care of her brothers and sisters?"

Violet heaved a dismal sigh. "That just doesn't seem fair."

"Fair or not, that's the way it is out here, honey. You gotta remember, we don't live by the same rules as city folks. We figure what's fair is whatever comes our way."

Despite what her mother had always told her, Violet frowned in disbelief. How could anyone look at life that way?

"Isn't there anyone Mr. Thurman can marry?" she asked.

"He did have his eye on Velma Campton for a while."

"Velma Campton?" Violet uttered the woman's name.

"She's a widow woman who lives in town. She's a seamstress of sorts, but she ain't nothin' like the fancy kind you got back in St. Louis. She just sews for folks who can't do for themselves, like Thurman. That's how he got to callin' on her." Ruth paused. "He came callin' twice, and both times she turned him down flat. Things didn't work out the way Thurman hoped they would."

"So he just gave up?" Violet asked, talking more to herself than to Ruth.

"I reckon if folks don't like what seems unfair, they can fight it, and sometimes they win. But Thurman ain't a fighter. He probably figured he got a fair chance at her."

Violet shook her head. It all sounded confusing to her.

What would it take to make them want to fight for what was right and deserving?

*   *   *

A few minutes passed; the only sound was that of the plodding horse. Violet lifted her face to the wind and liked the way it felt as it slithered through the strands of hair that had slipped from her chignon. Her mother would disapprove of her not wearing a bonnet and of the carefree manner in which the wagon jostled her about. Violet was consoled by the fact that the moment wouldn't last long.

She opened her mouth to say something then closed it. She took a deep breath to calm herself, but unable to hold back any longer, she blurted,

"Has Lance ever called on Lindsey?" There, it was done, she thought to herself. She hoped Ruth wouldn't think she was too forward.

Ruth considered the look on Violet's face and smiled knowingly. "Everyone in these parts has called on her, honey, but that girl's been sweet on Jed ever since they was kids."

Violet's heart swelled, taking her breath away until she felt weak and confused. She groaned as disconcerting thoughts ran through her mind. She had no right to feel envious of Lindsey. As for Lance, he was nothing more to her than a friend of her father's. It was true that he had saved her life, but that didn't give her the right to expect anything from him. If anything, she owed him something. But what? She had nothing but Tangleweed, and, after reading parts of her father's diary, it didn't appear to be anything that a person would want. Maybe she would feel differently if someone else had saved her life. It could have been Ralph Nolan. No, it wouldn't have mattered. Then why did she feel more than indebtedness? Why did she wonder if Lance thought of her instead of Lindsey? She shook off her thoughts. She wasn't here to think of what Lance Tridel meant to her. Violet reasoned that he probably never even gave her a second thought. If he wanted to call on Lindsey the rest of his life, that was his business. She deserved . . . .

An idea suddenly took hold. Even if she could never repay Lance, maybe she could do something to help Lindsey. The wheels of inspiration were spinning inside her head, moving faster than she could control them. She had made it to Texas, and now, with that same determination, she would find a way to give Lindsey the happiness she deserved.

Chapter Five

*L*ance loosened the reins he'd tied around the fence post, looped them around his horse's neck, and climbed slowly into his saddle. It was getting close to supper time, but he was in no hurry to get home. With the fence mending finished, he would have to ride around listening to the thunder that rumbled overhead if he wanted to be late for supper. His eyes level with the brim of his hat, Lance scanned the horizon and thought about the coming rain.

He felt at ease, knowing he could tell Aunt Ruth that he had wanted to get his work done before it rained. He leaned heavily into the saddle horn and complained under his breath. He knew he was bad off when he had to conjure up lame excuses to stay away from his own place to avoid a woman.

He still hadn't apologized to Violet for what the liveryman had said in Bartlett. It was hard for him to approach someone like Violet when he felt like a jack ass dragging his tail in the dust. He'd never been so hard on himself, but then, there had never been anyone like Violet Tippon.

Lance recalled that only a few hours ago, he'd been pretty sure of himself, making cocky remarks about eating crow, and then strutting off like a young stallion. That was before he saw Ralph Nolan galloping down Green Acre Road toward the Thurman place.

As soon as Nolan laid his beady eyes on Violet and started talking as if he were some sort of dude from back East, Lance knew he wouldn't stand a chance. If only Violet weren't mad because he'd boasted about getting married. Sometimes he just didn't know when to shut his mouth.

Lance sat up straight in his saddle. He opened his coat and pulled out a few sprigs topped with drooping blue and white flowers. He gazed at them tenderly then looked toward what was left of the setting sun. The wind stiffened, carrying with it a desolate, searching cry.

The remaining rays of sunlight stretched their golden shafts across the disappearing patches of blue sky. Lance felt his insides go weak. No matter how hard he tried, he couldn't quit seeing Violet's face, white and flawless as newly skimmed cream. Her flashing blue eyes were like dancing bluebonnets, and her hair was the color of a wild roan pony challenging the night wind. He knew he couldn't go on feeling like he did. Maybe tonight he could talk to her and set things straight.

Lance nudged his horse. "Come on, Shiner, gid up." The horse loped slow and easy across the open meadow through the windy dusk, seeming to sense that his owner was in no hurry to get home. Twilight came early as dove gray clouds laced with lavender spread thin veils over the sweeping sky.

It had already started to rain by the time Lance rode into the yard. It was a soft rain, just light enough to settle the dust and fill his nostrils with the smells of wet earth and grass. From the lighted windows, left open to cool the house, Lance recognized his uncle's shadow as he walked across the room. Seeing there wasn't a hired hand in sight, Lance figured supper had been over with for some time. Soon his aunt and uncle would be going out on the porch where they would sit and listen to the rain.

Lance dismounted and circled around to the front of his horse, tugging at the reins until Shiner followed him. Up at the house the screen door squeaked then banged shut, followed by the sound of footsteps crossing the porch.

"Is that you, Lance?"

"I'll be there in a minute, Aunt Ruth. Sorry I'm late. I had to finish up before it started rainin'."

There was a moment of silence mingled with the sound of rain forming puddles in the yard, followed by the sound of footsteps crossing back over the porch. The door squeaked open again. "I'll fix you a plate," Ruth said as she headed back inside, turning to look through the dark screen.

Ben walked up behind her and peered past her shoulder. "He's late tonight," he said.

"He's never been late before," Ruth replied in a low voice, her hands folded at her waist.

"I reckon he needs time to himself now and then. Nothin' to fret over."

Ruth's shoulders sagged as she turned around. "Nobody's frettin'. It just seems strange, that's all."

Ben watched her walk down the dimly lit hall to the kitchen, and he smiled and shook his head. She fretted over the boy whether she cared to admit it or not. He couldn't blame her, though; she had never had little ones of her own to fuss over. Ben opened the screen door and it patted shut when he stepped out onto the porch.

There were the sounds of boots on the steps and a few mumbled words before Ben sat in his chair and Lance headed toward the smell of food heating in the frying pan.

*   *   *

Violet was in her room writing a letter to her mother when she heard the screen door open and shut several times. Remembering that Ben wanted to talk to her about Tangleweed, she decided now was as good a time as any. She changed into a simple gourd skirt and a high—necked blouse made of white lawn with fitted sleeves that were slightly filled out at the shoulders. Gathering her hair, she twisted it and pinned it into a soft knot on the top of her head. Then she bent toward the mirror to take one last look at herself before she started down the stairs.

She could hear the drone of Lance's voice coming from the direction of the kitchen. The sizzling sound in the frying pan told her that Ruth was probably fixing him a late supper.

"Is that you, Miss Tippon?"

Violet followed the sound of Ben's voice. She opened the screen door and went out on the porch, softly shutting the door behind her. "The rain smells good," she said, as she sat in one of the rockers on the porch. The chair creaked softly on the wood floor before Ben replied.

"We ain't had this much rain in a coon's age. But then, that's the way it goes sometimes; no rain for months, sometimes even years, and then we git so much a body can't finish a day's work without gittin' drenched tryin'."

Violet sat quietly, wondering how long a coon's age was, and then wondering if it would rain so much that she wouldn't be able to go to Tangleweed in the morning.

"Ruth told me you were with my father the night he won Tangleweed in a card game," she began. "From what I've read in his diary, there doesn't seem to be much to the ranch. I wonder why someone would gamble over it."

"No doubt there's more to Tangleweed than your pa had a chance to write about 'fore he was killed. There was talk of gold on the place."

Violet stopped rocking. "I did read something about gold. But for some reason, Father didn't go into any details."

Ben leaned back, propping his chair against the house. He expanded his barrel-like chest and scratched it with both of his hands, and then rubbed his bristled chin so that it made a scratching sound. "If you're new to these parts, that gold story can be kinda deceivin'. Ya' see, there never was much gold to speak of in Texas, just talk 0' gold by fellas who had the fever so bad every rock that glittered was gonna make 'em rich. But, over the years, folks have claimed they found gold in a few places. More like findin' a gold tooth in a dead man's mouth, if you ask me. But then, no one's asked me till you come along." He let out a tired groan and dropped his chair to the floor. "Anyway, they got all kinds of wild stories to go with their claims, and Tangleweed's just one of 'em."

"Do you know if my father ever found any gold?" Violet asked in a quiet, uncertain voice.

"Sure." Ben nodded. "You probably don't know this, but Tangleweed's what brought your pa to Texas in the first place. The way he told it, he was on one of them riverboats—same one I was on. It was there he heard a man braggin' 'bout a place his pa owned in Texas. Since your pa was aimin' to head this way someday, it gave him the opportunity he'd been lookin' for."

"Do you think there's still gold on Tangleweed?" Violet asked in a more steady voice.

Ben released a contemplative sigh. "Well, it's hard to say. I have my doubts, and yet I saw what little gold your pa dug outta that claim." He paused. "Your pa staked his life on the fact that there was gold for the pickin' along them creeks out there."

There was a brief silence; then Violet asked, "Did you know the man on the riverboat?"

"Well now," Ben projected, "the way I see it, I could say 'yes' and stir up a whole can O' worms. Ya' might go to thinkin' your pa was killed outta spite or revenge. All I can tell ya', and ya' might already know this, is that the man who lost Tangleweed to your pa is dead. The one we all been wonderin' about is his son. We figure he wants what he thinks rightfully belongs to him, and. . ."

Violet interrupted. "And you think his son's the one who tried to kill me?"

"I reckon ya' got me there, ma'am. I'd have to say 'yes' to that question and hope and pray I'm wrong."

Violet sat trembling in the dark, her fingers laced tightly in her lap. Out of nowhere, a dark figure appeared at the foot of the porch steps. Before she was able to catch herself, she gasped.

Her being startled didn't seem to alarm Ben. He stood up slowly and easily, shoving the tips of his fingers into his hip pockets. "What'cha doin' out on a night like this, Doc?"

A tall, lanky man, slightly stooped at the shoulders, stepped up onto the porch and removed his hat, nodding his head briefly in Violet's direction. "I've been over at Thurman's place. I figured since I was in the neighborhood, I'd drop by to see how Miss Tippon was gettin' along."

Violet started to get up, but the doctor raised his hand in protest. "Don't bother yourself none, ma'am. I won't be stayin'. I just like to keep track of my patients, to make sure they're doin' all right."

Violet settled back in the rocker. "Then it'll please you to know I'm doing just fine. I appreciate your stopping by."

"She's a real lady, ain't she, Doc?" Ben asked proudly.

"Wouldn't hurt us none if she stayed around," the doctor answered. "Ol' Tippon sure would'a been proud of her."

The door creaked open. "I been tryin' to talk her into stayin', but she's a woman after her pa's own heart," Ruth said from the wavy shadows cast by the lamp Lance was hanging on a nail to the side of the door.

"We was just talkin' about Tangleweed," Ben added.

Ruth crossed her arms over her bosom. "I s'pose Violet told ya' what a fool Nolan was makin' of himself today over at Thurman's place, and how he's comin' over in the mornin' to take her to Tangleweed."

Violet opened her mouth to protest when all at once Lance loomed in the full glare of the yellow lamp light. "You can't go to Tangleweed with him," he protested.

"And why not?" Violet challenged, her hands gripping the arms of her chair while her back stiffened.

Lance shot a glance at Ben, and then at Ruth. Quickly dismissing the 'fox in the hen house' look on his aunt's face, he looked back at Violet, whose eyes remained fixed on him.

"It's not safe to go, that's why."

"You mean with Mr. Nolan?"

"I mean with anyone," Lance shot back. "Not now, anyway."

Violet sprang to her feet, her chin protruding, her hands clenched at her sides. "But that's why I came to Wood River—to go to Tangleweed."

"Maybe it'd be best if they found your pa's killer first," Ruth suggested.

A stern look captured Lance's face. "Aunt Ruth, if ya' don't mind, I'd like to talk to Miss Tippon alone for a moment. It'll only be a minute, Uncle Ben."

"I'd best be goin'," the doctor said, placing his hat firmly on his head and turning toward the sound of the rain.

"I don't mean to run ya' off, Doc," Lance apologized. "There's a few things here that need straightenin' out, that's all."

"No need to explain, son. I was fixin' to go anyway."

Ben and Ruth said their good-byes to the doctor as they walked through the doorway. Ruth shut the heavy inside door.

The instant they were alone, Lance gripped Violet's arm and drew her toward him. Standing face to face, Violet's knees shook uncontrollably while Lance's heart was pounding like a million stampeding mustangs. His warning words echoed in Violet's ears until she was barely able to discern what he was saying.

"I refuse to let you go to Tangleweed tomorrow."

Violet fought against Lance's hold. "How dare you speak to me in that . . ."

"You have no idea what you're getting yourself into," Lance persisted, "and I don't have time to go trailing after you."

"Why, you impertinent cowpuncher! You have no right . . ." Violet's hand flew toward Lance's face but he snatched it in mid air.

"Am I goin' to have to tie you up to keep you from swingin' at me all the time?"

"Let me go," Violet scolded in a low, angry voice, hoping that Ben and Ruth were at the other end of the house. She knew that more than likely they were standing just on the other side of the door.

Lance studied her face in the soft light of the lamp. "The boys and I made a little wager, and it looks like I came out on the winnin' side."

"What are you talking about?" Violet demanded, in as brusque a manner as she could with Lance standing so close to her.

"Your eyes are the color of bluebonnets," he whispered hoarsely.

Violet tugged in an effort to get away, which only served to tighten Lance's hold on her. "What's a bluebonnet?" she snapped.

"It's a Texas wildflower," he said in a contemplative voice.

Violet's curt reply was swept aside, when he suddenly bent down and kissed her lips.

*   *   *

Lance couldn't sleep that night thinking about how many times he wanted to kick himself for doing what he did. He didn't know what had come over him. Something inside of him had told him that if he didn't kiss Violet, then and there, he might never get the chance. The blame thing of it was, he still hadn't apologized for what he'd said to the livery man in Bartlett.

Lance knew one thing was sure: Violet was Sam Tippon's daughter, through and through, besides being as beautiful and fierce as the land itself. He had never seen a woman so full of fight and determination. She was just the kind of gal he liked, full of fire and spunk. He thought about what had happened after he kissed Violet. He had no sooner let go of her when she was trying her damndest to wallop him one more time. He finally told her he'd kiss her again if she didn't stop trying to floor him. He smiled when he recalled the way she threw back her shoulders and glared at him, before she marched inside the house, slamming the door as hard as she could. She was so mad he could hear her stomping all the way up the stairs.

When all was quiet, Lance had heard his aunt, through the open window, talking to his uncle in a muffled voice, saying now they knew what had been ailing him. After that, he decided he'd rather sleep in the bunkhouse than go inside and answer a lot of silly questions.

After tossing and turning all night, Lance felt exhausted when he dragged himself out of bed at what he thought was sunrise. He looked at the crude walls and the unkempt bunks, scratching his head and yawning until it dawned on him why he was the only one there. All at once, he was wide awake and flying out of his bunk and into his clothes. He knew it had to be past sunup. All the men were gone, and he'd never even heard them stir. He tore open the door and dashed across the yard, grumbling angrily to himself as he leapt up the back steps to the house and stomped noisily into the kitchen.

"Well, what do we have here?" Ruth asked, without taking her eyes off of the biscuit dough she was rolling out on the floured table.

Lance shoved his shirttails into his pants. "Why didn't someone wake me up?"

"When ya' didn't get up, we figured you was ailin'."

Lance groaned, "Did Violet go with Nolan?"

"They left 'bout a half hour ago."

"Didn't you try to stop her?"

"I tried, but she's a bit stubborn."

Lance took a chunk of bread from a loaf on a cutting board and shoved it into his mouth.

"Now you just sit down here, and I'll fix you a proper breakfast," Ruth said, motioning with the rolling pin.

"I can't. I've got to make it to Tangleweed before they do."

"And how are you gonna manage that?"

"I'll go along Boot Creek Road. It comes out near Tippon's place."

Ruth stopped rolling dough and looked up at Lance, her brows bent into a frown. "What are you fixin' to do, Lance Tridel?"

"Keep an eye on Nolan, that's what."

"What makes you think you have any say where that girl's concerned?"

"Nobody'd know the answer to that question better than you, unless it was Uncle Ben," Lance replied.

Ruth pursed her lips. "It wasn't our fault you was talkin' so loud."

Lance quickly glanced at Ruth from the corner of his eye then shoved another hunk of bread into his mouth. "No matter, Nolan's up to no good, and he's not gonna get away with it this time."

"Now, don't you go causin' any trouble; do'ya hear me?" Ruth scolded.

"I don't plan to. But someone has to keep an eye on that girl. She's too headstrong for her own good."

Lance didn't see Ruth's subtle smile as he darted out the door, toward the stable to saddle his horse.

*   *   *

On the way to Tangleweed, Violet watched the downy white clouds sailing across the blue sky, casting flat shadows over the land as they played a game of hide and seek with the sun. The previous night's rain left the fresh morning air sweeping lazy billows over the countryside.

Nolan had brought a gentle horse for Violet to ride, since getting to her father's claim meant traveling through some untamed country. As she rocked gently in the saddle, she found herself thinking how totally free and easy life was away from the city. It was going to be hard to go back to St. Louis when the time came.

"You're on Tangleweed land now," Nolan said, turning halfway in his saddle and flinging his arm out to indicate what lay ahead.

Violet scanned the wild, ruthless acres before her. She was forced to admit that Texas was a man's country, and Tangleweed, despite its beauty, had nothing to offer her except some idea of what her father had been searching for.

Nolan pulled on his reins and both horses stopped. He turned, leaning against the back of his saddle, and looked curiously at Violet's face.

"You think you might be interested in selling Tangleweed, Miss Tippon?"

Violet looked away, shading her eyes from the growing brightness of the sun. "I don't know. I suppose I should hold on to it a while. It's really all I have left of my father."

The horses pawed at the rocky path and tossed their heads, which caused the harnesses to clink. "Whoa there," Nolan repeated firmly until the horses were quiet. Looking back at Violet, he said, "It sounds like you might be staying in Wood River for a while, then."

"Well, at least until I've had a chance to look over Tangleweed."

"That might take some time. As you can see for yourself, Tangleweed's a big place."

Violet wasn't sure if she saw Nolan wince or if the glaring sun had played a trick on her eyes, but suddenly he seemed different. He was sitting straight, with his shoulders held back stiffly, his furtive eyes studying something in the distance. When he looked at her, his eyes filled with an expression she couldn't interpret.

"Did you know that my father once owned this land?" he asked in a low contemplative voice.

Stunned, Violet shook her head and mumbled an insignificant reply.

"I'd be more than willing to buy the place back from you, whenever, and if ever you should decide to sell. I'd offer you a fair price, enough for you to live on for years."

"Well, I . . . don't know," Violet stammered.

"Miss Tippon, it might be a good idea for you to make up your mind. Someone's already tried to stop you from claiming it. You never know what might happen if you should decide not to sell."

A rush of fear engulfed Violet and her heart began to race uncontrollably. What was he trying to say? He couldn't be the man that Ben had told her about . . . the man on the riverboat. Surely Ruth would have said something when she told her that she was going to Tangleweed with Nolan. Violet swallowed hard. "And what if I'm not ready to make up my mind?" she challenged.

"The way a lawyer would see it, you being Sam Tippon's only heir, if you should happen to die, then Tangleweed would rightfully belong to me. I have witnesses to prove that Tangleweed belonged to my father in the first place, and no legal transaction was ever exchanged when your father acquired it. There was nothing but a hand-shake."

Violet's shoulders squared, though she tried to keep her face as expressionless as possible. "Are you saying that Tangleweed belongs to you, and that I have no rightful claim to it? Because if you are . . ."

Violet's words were cut off by the sharp ping of a bullet that whizzed by her face and struck the jagged rocks behind her. She gasped, her eyes fixed on Nolan, who was quickly scanning the hills a short distance away. He looked frantically at Violet then whipped out his gun. All at once a bullet from the opposite direction clipped his hand, and he let out a pained cry while his gun went flying through the air.

"Violet! Get away, fast!"

Lance's warning reverberated in Violet's ears as she quickly scanned the terrain, searching for Lance. She glanced back at Nolan and the look on his face charged her with fear. Tightening her grip on the reins, she jabbed her heels into the horse's flanks. Her horse broke into a swift, hard gallop. Violet charged over the rocky hillside without thinking twice about who was following at her heels. She could hear Nolan calling for her to stop, but her only concern was to make it back to the Rough and Tumble alive.

Violet had never ridden so hard and fast in all her life, and by the time she reached the Tridel ranch, she was overcome by heat. Her hair, which she had taken such pains to put up properly, was hanging limply to one side; her hat was barely on her head. She dropped to the ground just as Lance's horse rapidly came up behind her, stirring a whirlwind of dust. Lance swung from his saddle, slapped the gelding's flank then strode with angry determination toward Violet.

"Are you trying to get yourself killed?" Lance hollered. Then, seeing how mad Violet was, he decided he'd keep his distance until he had a chance to explain why he had followed her to Tangleweed.

Violet stood still, her fists clenched at her sides, her eyes flashing defiantly at Lance, who, although standing a ways from her, was big enough to block out the glare of the sun. She whisked a strand of hair from her smudged forehead and angrily spouted, "What do you think you're doing? You had no right to follow me."

"I did if I thought you were in danger, and it appears to me you were."

"What are you talking about? How do I know you weren't the one trying to shoot at me?"

Lance's face darkened. "If it had been me, I'd have been shootin' at Nolan, not at you; and I wouldn't have missed, either."

Bewildered, Violet asked, "Why in the world would you want to shoot Ralph Nolan?"

Lance yanked his hat off and heaved a frustrated sigh. "I didn't say I wanted to shoot him. I said if I was the one doin' the shootin', I'd have been shootin' at him, not at you. And I wouldn't have had to shoot twice," he stated, a quick nod indicating his certainty.

"You think he killed my father, don't you?"

"I didn't say that."

"But that's what you think. That's why you followed us, and why you shot at him. I suppose you think he was going to kill me, too."

Lance gave a quick nod. "What I think is that he's not one to be trusted."

"The problem with you is that you're jealous of him."

Lance crossed his arms and smiled contemplatively. "You sure do get yourself into some unlikely predicaments, Miss Tippon."

"You go right ahead and think what you like, Mr. Tridel, but you're wrong about Mr. Nolan. He wasn't the man in Bartlett who kidnapped me. That man was much taller."

"Nolan could've sent someone to do the job."

"If he wanted to kill me, then why did he offer to buy Tangleweed?"

The screen door slammed shut. "What's all the ruckus about?"

Lance and Violet looked at Ruth, who ambled across the yard wiping her hands on her apron.

Before Lance could open his mouth, Violet blurted, "Lance thinks Mr. Nolan was trying to kill me."

"Lance Tridel! What's gotten into you?" Ruth scolded.

Lance's shoulders squared defiantly. "I never said that!" he bellowed.

Ruth looked at Violet and shook her head. "If you don't look a sight. You both look like a couple 0' misfits."

"Well, she'd have looked a whole lot worse than that if I'd have found her dead," Lance replied as he walked over to the water trough. He dipped his hat in the cool water, then bent to pour it over his head. He came up gasping and slapped his hat against his thigh. "Somebody took a shot at her, and she thinks it was me."

"You did shoot at Mr. Nolan," Violet huffed.

"He was goin' for his gun. How did I know what he was gonna do?"

"Who was goin' for his gun?" Ben questioned, walking out of the shed with a spade and a hoe over his shoulder.

Ruth tossed her head toward the squabbling pair. "Lance here thinks Nolan was fixin' to shoot Violet."

"Not until someone took a pot shot at her from the hills and missed," Lance was quick to add.

"Well, if that don't beat all," Ben said calmly as he walked over to the water trough. He laid aside the tools then reached inside his shirt pocket and pulled out a thin, paper sheath filled with cigarette paper. After wetting the tip of his finger, he took out a fine sheet of paper and slipped the container back into his pocket. He worked a small leather pouch of tobacco out of his pants pocket and pulled it open with his teeth. Without lifting his head, he glanced up at Violet. "If you don't mind my askin', Miss Tippon, what do you plan to do with Tangleweed now that you've seen the place?"

Chapter Six

A perplexed look came over Violet's face as she studied Ben, who was now tipping the tobacco pouch above the funneled paper. He carefully tapped a line of tobacco into the paper until it was filled. Then with the string between his teeth, he closed the bag and again glanced at Violet, which told her he was waiting for her answer.

Feeling somewhat defeated, Violet removed her hat, pushed the hair away from her face, and sighed wearily. "I don't know," Violet said woefully. "I never really got a chance to see the place, or even set foot in my father's cabin before someone shot at me. That's when I heard Lance shouting from out of nowhere to . . ."

Ben raised a silencing hand, his head shaking from side to side. "We already been over all that." He took a deep breath and released it. "I reckon it's time we laid our cards out on the table and put an end to all the mystery once and for all." He took his time clearing the gravely sound from his throat before he said, "Some folks 'round here think Nolan killed your pa." He scratched his jaw then, drew a wooden match out of his shirt pocket. Striking it on the side of the water trough, he lit his mangled cigarette. For a lingering moment, he peered at Violet through an ascending trail of wavy blue smoke. "They say he did it 'cause he thinks Tangleweed rightfully belongs to him."

When Violet grimaced Ben quickly added, "It's like I told you before. I was there the night your pa won Tangleweed fair and square from Nolan's pa. They shook hands on it and then parted company."

"Mr. Nolan told me there was nothing signed to prove that my father owned Tangleweed. He said legally it belongs to him."

56

"'Round here, a handshake's as good as one of them there signed documents they hand out in the city." Ben paused to consider. "What you gotta keep in mind, ma'am, is that even though things are prett'n'ere tame where you come from, it's a lot different out here. Why, everything's wild in Texas—from the sun risin' to those wild flowers Ruth puts in them cannin' jars on the table. Nothin's tame that don't wanna be tamed, and your pa didn't wanna be tamed. That's why some folks didn't take to him and why they believe he cheated on his hand."

Violet's shoulders dropped, her arms falling limp at her sides. "But you said he was an honest man and everyone liked him."

Through slit eyes, Ben looked over at Lance and then at the cigarette that was clamped between his dirt-stained finger and thumb. "Everyone but the Nolans," he said decidedly.

"You mean because of the card game?" Violet quizzed.

Ruth nudged closer to Violet. "No one started talkin' against your pa till he showed up one day with a bag 0' gold nuggets, everyone the size of a man's eyetooth. That's when Nolan started . . ." Ruth stopped short as though she had said too much.

Ben patted Ruth's forearm to show that she was on the right track. "Like I said last night, Nolan's pa is dead, but it ain't no secret Nolan wants the land back."

"But why would Mr. Nolan offer to buy Tangleweed from me if he was the one who was trying to kill me?" Violet asked.

"By offering, you wouldn't suspect him of killing your pa, or of trying to kill you," Lance said.

All at once the reality of the day's events struck her, and Violet shuddered before uttering a weak reply. "You knew all of this, and you let me go with him anyway?"

"I tried to stop you," Lance said, his words reproving her.

"Now, Lance," Ruth remarked, putting a comforting hand on Violet's arm. Ruth looked at her and spoke in a more sympathetic voice. "There was no way I could of convinced you after the way that insufferable man was carryin' on yesterday over at Thurman's place."

A series of images flashed through Violet's mind as she tried to make some sense out of what she was hearing. The whole story was like a complicated puzzle scattered over a table with none of the pieces fitting to make a picture. She wondered if Ralph Nolan had offered to buy Tangleweed from her father. If so, why hadn't her father sold it back to him? It was hard for her to comprehend why someone would kill an old man for land that could have been bar—gained over. Her father had only gotten a small amount of gold out of the claim. Confused, Violet shook her head. There had to be some other reason why he wouldn't give up Tangleweed.

"I just don't know." She shrugged. "There's still no proof that Ralph Nolan had anything to do with my father's death, or if he was the man who tried to kill me. All anyone has to go on is the fact that his family disliked my father."

"That's why nothin's been done up to now," Ben said. "But at least you know the whole story."

Violet raised her eyes in thought. She decided she would spend the rest of the day reading her father's diary. She would forget about what to do with Tangleweed until she had a chance to spend some time there by herself.

The thought had no sooner left her when the sound of a fast-approaching horse diverted everyone's attention. It was Nolan, riding like someone was hot on his heels.

"Whoa! Whoa, there!" His horse skidded to a halt sending up a cloud of dust around his stirrups. Violet bent her head to keep the dust from her face, and she noticed that Nolan's boots were caked with fresh mud and grass. Earlier they had been painstakingly rubbed to a fine polish. She quickly thought back over their trek to Tangleweed. Nowhere could she recall the horses going through mud.

"Stay right where you're at," Lance commanded, whipping out his gun. He flipped back the hammer and Nolan readily obeyed. No one made an effort to stop Lance's threat.

Nolan's hands went up. One was bound with a bloody strip torn from the hem of his shirt that hung loosely at his waist. "Now, hold on there. I don't know what's going on here. I just came by to tell you I found the guy who took a pot shot at Miss Tippon."

"Where is he then?" Lance jeered, his eyes fixed hard on Nolan.

"He wasn't too cooperative. I had to tie him to a tree down near Prospect Hill. I wanted to catch up with you."

"You seem pretty willin' to help out," Ben said with as much calm as he could muster.

"And why shouldn't I? For all I know, he could've been shooting at me and just missed."

"I take it you won't mind then if Lance helps you corral this here fella and rides in with you to see the sheriff."

Violet had been watching Nolan carefully and, although it was barely noticeable, she was certain she saw his left eye twitch.

"Suit yourself," he said, slowly lowering his hands, his eyes fixed on Lance's gun as Lance released the hammer. Nolan looked over at Violet.

"I'm sorry about what happened," he said, cautiously reaching for the reins.

Violet watched Lance cross the yard to the stable before she turned her attention to Nolan. "Thank you, Mr. Nolan, but it wasn't your fault."

"You didn't get to see much of Tangleweed," he said. "If you'd like . . ."

"I think you'd better leave now," Ruth said, with a touch of contempt in her voice as she shoved her clenched hands into the pockets of her big apron.

A stern look covered Ben's face, his angry eyes locked on Nolan. He saw Lance riding out of the stable and he picked up the reins of the horse that Violet had been riding and handed them to Nolan. In a less than tolerant voice, he said, "We're mighty obliged to ya' for capturin' that scoundrel. Let him know that I'll be in to meet him in the mornin'."

Nolan looked back at Violet and nodded his head in departure. He whipped his reins around, and he and Lance rode out of the yard at a brisk canter.

*   *   *

The afternoon wore on while Violet stayed in her room reading her father's diary. Having left the door open, she could hear Ruth patting about the house, humming to herself, and the sound of a wooden spoon thudding steadily against a crock bowl. Violet smiled to herself when she pictured Ruth with the bowl cradled in the crook of her sturdy arm.

After a short time, Violet heard Ruth calling Ben, who was working in the yard. Violet figured he was staying close to the house until Lance came back. The oven door creaked twice then the screen door banged, and Violet heard Ruth ask Ben where he'd put the gardening tools.

"Ya' mean you called me all the way in here just to ask me where I put the dadgum garden tools?" Ben growled, the words sounding throughout the house.

"Well, if you'd put 'em back where they belong, I wouldn't have to send out a search party every time I wanna till the garden," Ruth retorted.

The back door banged and Violet got up and looked out the window. Ben and Ruth were outside searching around the tool shed, the barn, and the hen house. Finally, they stomped back inside and Violet heard Ben say:

"I remember now. A few days ago, when it started to look like rain, I put em' in the springhouse."

"It's too late to till the garden now," Violet heard Ruth complain. "I might as well go after the cows so you can start milkin', or supper'll be later than it already is."

"Then what'd ya' call me in for?" Ben bellowed.

Violet scampered down the stairs and fluttered into the kitchen. "I'll go after the cows," she said, out of breath.

Ben and Ruth stopped what they were doing and eyed her curiously.

"You sure you know what you're fixin' to do?" Ruth asked.

Violet quickly nodded. "When I was twelve, I spent the summer at my aunt and uncle's, and they had cows."

Ruth's brows bent. "Well . . ."

"Oh, let her go," Ben said in a kindly voice. "It might do her some good to get out." He motioned with a slight toss of his head. "They're out in the south pasture. They like the wild clover down near the stream."

"Like I was gonna say," Ruth huffed, nudging Ben in the side with her elbow, "if you think you can handle it, I'll get to startin' on supper."

Violet was all smiles. She smoothed out the folds of her simple calico dress and brushed back the strands of hair that had slipped from her braid that was wrapped around the crown of her head.

"This ain't nothin' like goin' on a picnic," Ruth said, concerned when she saw how excited Violet was.

Ben smiled whimsically. "You go on now, and don't you worry none about the cows. They'll come along real easy like."

The screen door banged shut and Violet was gone.

Standing side by side in the doorway, Ben and Ruth watched her go off into the dusky sunlight without her bonnet.

"She sure looks purtty in that frilly dress," Ruth mused, "with her face flushed and all."

"That color reminds me of the wild plums growin' down by the springhouse," Ben added.

They both sighed softly.

"Somethin's different 'bout her from when she first came here," Ben said.

"She ain't so citified no more," Ruth said.

Ben nodded. "She reminds me of a young sapling that belongs out in the open prairie." He paused. "It'd be nice if she was to stay around a while. She kinda livens up the place."

Ruth turned and faded into the shadows down the length of the hall leading to the kitchen. "You'd stand a better chance 0' seein' that storm cellar dug out all by itself than seein' that girl stay 'round for much longer if Lance don't get a better handle on things."

"I reckon I could put a bug in his ear," Ben muttered as he opened the screen door. The door creaked softly when Ben closed it. He made his way to the springhouse to get the garden tools to return them to the shed.

*　　*　　*

There were only four cows. Violet saw them as soon as she closed the pasture gate and started up the footpath, which took her over a gentle rise dotted with sleepy wildflowers. The sun was nearly set, but there was still plenty of light to see by. She wrapped her arms around her shoulders; deeply breathed in the soft, drowsy breeze of early dusk; and, for some reason, thought about her mother, who was so far away. All at once she had a feeling of deep regret or misgiving, and realized she would miss Texas when the time came for her to go home.

Violet had finished reading her father's diary, and even though Nolan had offered to buy Tangleweed from her father, her father clung to it with the belief that he would someday strike the mother lode. Other than that, he wrote little of the small spread or of gold. Mostly he recorded how happy he was living in the wide-open country under the stars and the clouds pushed along by gentle, laid back breezes. Violet knew now that it wasn't her mother he left behind; it was the life he had been forced to live in St. Louis. He had never been a city man, though he had tried, for her mother's sake. Violet saw that as a tender gesture. She realized she shouldn't really blame him for leaving, but the fact remained; he had not only left her mother, he had left her as well, searing her mother's heart. For that reason it was hard for Violet to forgive.

Her thoughts were interrupted by a loud, bawling sound. She peered across the prairie grass and saw the spotted cows ambling slowly toward her. Just off the road from where the cows were, she saw a man on horseback making his way through the grassy meadow. She cautiously watched him until he drew closer, and she saw that it was Lance returning to the ranch.

Lance had just been wondering if it was Violet's chestnut-colored hair or her soft, blue eyes that caused him to be so taken with her. Hearing the cows bawl, he looked up and saw her standing in the middle of a blanket of nodding wildflowers, the cows lulling about her. The faint light of early dusk surrounding her reflected a quiet beauty he had not yet seen in her.

All at once her quick temper paled in comparison. He quickly wondered how he should approach her and what he could say so that he wouldn't appear to be a blundering fool. He didn't put much stock in flattery and smooth words, so he just said what was on his mind.

"I never figured on seeing you up here," he said, nudging his horse closer.

Violet turned her head. "I thought it might help if I went after the cows. That way your aunt wouldn't have to do it."

Lance laughed softly as he dismounted. "Looks like they forgot to tell ya' those cows won't follow unless they know ya'."

Frowning softly, Violet looked across the sloping meadow to where the house stood. It looked small and insignificant, as though it was made out of match sticks. "No, they never mentioned it," she replied.

"I'd say ya' could probably use a little help, and since they're used to me, it looks like I came along at just the right time."

Violet's eyes clouded. She gripped the fullness of her skirts and started walking across the meadow, her steps awkward and unsteady as she lifted her feet above the tall grass.

"Where ya' goin'?"

"You put them up to this, didn't you?" Violet called over her shoulder.

"If that don't beat all. How was I suppose to know ya' was goin' after the cows?" Lance dismounted and made his way through the wildflowers until he was at her side. He took hold of her arm and she turned with a start.

He let go of her then backed away. "I didn't mean to scare ya'. I just wanted to talk to ya', that's all."

"About what?" Violet quickly retorted.

"I been meanin' to say I was sorry about what the liveryman said back in Bartlett. If I hadn't a been such a . . . a blowhard, you wouldn't a had all the problems you been havin'."

Violet felt ashamed at having thought Lance was going to kiss her again. To her, he seemed arrogant one minute, and the next minute, he was like a little boy caught with his hand in the cookie jar. She smiled faintly up at him.

"I accept your apology, but what happened in Bartlett was my own fault. If I hadn't run off the way I did, I never would've met up with that man. I just want to try and forget it."

Lance bent down, picked a flower, and started twirling the stem between his fingers. "It seems like you've seen nothing but the bad side of Texas."

A moment of silence slipped between them. Violet stood with her arms crossed, staring at the meadow where the flowers were starting to bend with the stiff night breeze. "I thought it would be so easy—just come out here, take a look at Tangleweed, sell the place, and go back home. But things just keep getting more complicated."

"Well, Nolan did say he'd buy Tangleweed. Maybe you'd like to take him up on it."

"I don't know. Something tells me I'm not ready to sell, but I can't stay here forever."

"Why not? This isn't really such a bad place to live."

"But you're used to it here. It's where you grew up. Besides, my mother's back in St. Louis."

"Actually, I lived near Ft. Worth until I was 10. I lived with my parents in a white house with gables, and I went to a school in town."

"Why did you move to Wood River?"

"I came here with Uncle Ben and Aunt Ruth . . . after my folks were killed during a bank holdup."

Violet's doleful eyes fixed on Lance. "I'm sorry, I didn't know."

"There's no need to be sorry; it was a long time ago."

"Do you remember what happened?"

Lance plucked the petals from the flower stem and watched them sail into the grass. "I was in the general store lookin' over the pocketknives. My pa had promised to buy one for my birthday. Anyway, my parents went to the bank. They said they'd be right back, but they never came . . ."

"If you don't want to talk about it . . ."

"I've never talked about it with anyone before." Lance paused, and Violet found herself wanting him to continue to confide in her.

"Then I'm glad you told me," she said softly.

Lance tossed aside the bare stem. "I don't remember much of anything after that. The store was dark. I heard gunfire, so I ran and hid behind the counter. I was crouched real low with my hands over my head, but I could still hear people runnin' along the boardwalk and horses galloping. People were shoutin'. There was a lot of confusion." Lance exhaled, his shoulders drooped. "The funeral was a few days later. Now when I think about it, all I did was stand there, lookin' up at Aunt Ruth, who was dressed in black, and wonderin' why she was carryin' on so." He took off his hat and drew his hand across his brow as though trying to wipe away the picture his words had formed. "The next day we got on the train. I was so happy; I'd never been on a train before."

Violet fought back the lump that ached in her throat and the burning tears blinding her eyes. She thought about how lonely she had been over the years; always wondering what kind of man her father was, wishing that he would come home, and yet Lance had suffered a far greater loss and perhaps a deeper loneliness.

Unafraid, Violet put her hand out and touched one of the cow's soft flanks. With her heart pounding in her throat, her voice cracked. "It was hard for you, wasn't it? I mean, being without them and all?"

To her surprise, he shook his head. "At first it was. I used to cry myself to sleep, wonderin' when they were gonna come and take me back home. But time passed, and Uncle Ben and Aunt Ruth made it up to me. They loved me more than I deserved to be loved at times . . ."

Violet could no longer hold back the tears that streamed down her face. When Lance saw she was crying, he dropped his hat and grabbed her in his arms, holding her tightly against him. She was just like one of the wildflowers that bent at his feet. He wanted desperately to protect her from anything or anyone that might harm her.

"Don't cry," he whispered softly into her scented hair until her cries were mere whimpers against his shoulder. The supper bell clanged and the cows lowed, one right after another. The birds chirped softly as they settled in for the night while Lance and Violet's silhouettes remained etched against the faded purple sky.

*   *   *

Little was said when Lance and Violet came walking through the door a while later. The house was filled with the noise of hired hands leaving the cluttered table. Their heavy boots clomped and their spurs clinked like the music of a player piano, the lyrics being their loud laughter and belches they no longer sought to conceal.

Ruth was stacking the dishes, pretending not to notice that Lance and Violet were quiet and unsure of what to do with themselves. She asked them how far the cows had strayed and, without waiting for a reply, said she would fix up a plate of food for them. Ben was sitting in his chair next to the lamp, pretending to look through the Rancher's Report, when he asked, in a lazy drawl, about the man Nolan claimed to have captured.

Lance pulled a chair away from the table, swung his leg over the back, and was seated. "It appears he got away," he answered, around a mouthful of food.

Disgusted, Ben let the paper fall in his lap. "Don't surprise me one bit," he grumbled.

Roscoe, the last hired hand to leave the table, started toward the door. "He's a rough character if you ask me," he said. He picked up his hat and, with his hand on the door knob, turned and asked Ben if he still wanted the boys to go after the mustangs that were holed up near Silver Springs.

Before Ben even had a chance to open his mouth, Lance shot up out of his chair as if he was ready to go at that moment. "You bet! Tell the boys to be ready at sunrise day after tomorrow, or they'll be left behind. As soon as I tie up some loose ends, I'll be ready to head out. And tell Skeeter to lay off the bottle for a couple of days or he'll be diggin' post holes instead of ridin' out."

A toothless grin covered Roscoe's face, his eyes bright with excitement. He pulled his hat down over his brow, and his face almost disappeared beneath its wide brim. He quickly inclined his head in Violet's direction then stomped out.

All at once the house was quiet. Only the clattering of the dishes, Ruth insisted on doing by herself broke the silence.

"I'm goin' into town tomorrow; you can ride along if you're feelin' up to it," Ruth said to Violet, who was at the table arranging the doily and the canning jar filled with flowers.

"I'd like that. I should send a letter to my mother, and if you don't mind taking me, I think I'd like to stop and visit with the seamstress."

Ruth cocked her head sideways and smiled at Violet, who had a curious twinkle in her eye. It's hard tellin' just what that girl's up to, Ruth thought to herself.

Since they had a busy day planned for tomorrow, Violet announced she was going to bed, using the excuse that she was tired. Ruth saw how Lance looked puppy-eyed at Violet, even though Violet avoided his trailing eyes.

After she climbed the stairs, aware that Lance had been watching her, Violet leaned against her bedroom door and heaved an exhaustive sigh. The evening had put more strain on her than she cared to think about.

She closed her eyes and felt the cool breeze that puffed the curtains. A moment passed before she began to hear rain dripping slowly from the eaves outside her window. She looked outside and hoped it wouldn't be a heavy downpour.

Violet dimmed the lamp and started to undress. She slipped a cambric nightgown over her head, sat on the edge of the bed, and unbraided her hair, distracted by the fluttering inside of her. She sighed heavily, thinking she shouldn't have allowed Lance to hold her the way he did. She knew it was wrong, and yet she made no effort to stop him. She would be going home soon, the thought of which pained her. There was no place in St. Louis for Lance Tridel. He was like one of the mustangs Roscoe had asked about, even the mention of which set Lance's eyes aglow and his spirit soaring. Lance thrived on being free, spurred on by a sudden and unexpected recklessness, never having been confined the way Violet had been for most of her life. Though saddened once by tragedy, his very being was full of laughter and wild daring, like the boundless wind and the untamed wilderness she now lay awake listening to at night.

She blew out the lamp and climbed between the crisp sheets. The house was dark and quiet, and she felt alone. Violet knew she could never ask Lance to leave Texas. A sob escaped her. No one had ever held her the way Lance had. Since being in Wood River, she had known the simple delights of feeling the wind in her hair and smelling the scent of wildflowers. She closed her eyes, her lips pressed tightly together as she scolded herself for ever wanting to change him. All she could do now was sell Tangleweed and leave before the thought of going back to St. Louis became unbearable.

Having somewhat consoled herself, she lay in the darkness listening to the murmur of voices on the front porch. Later that night, after everyone had gone to bed, the sound of footsteps having faded on the stairs, she listened to the rain as it washed across the night sky.

Chapter Seven

O n the way to town the next morning, Ruth told Violet about the "quiltin'" and the picnic on Saturday at the Thurman's home.

"I been meanin' to say somethin' about it before this, but with so much goin' on and all, it just slipped my mind," Ruth explained. "When someone dies, the ladies take the deceased one's clothes, cut them into squares, and piece them together to make a quilt for the family to use. It consoles them, havin' somethin' to remember them by. We've been doin' it for years."

Violet thought how comforting it must be to the family to be surrounded by people who cared. Even though very few people knew her, in a small way she would be comforted, too, since she had lost her father.

Wood River seemed to have been quickly put together, appearing to be a coarse town, though it was quaint in many respects. Discarded kettles and worn-out coffee pots full of flowers had been placed on the boardwalks along the storefronts. The names of the establishments had been painstakingly outlined in muted shades of red and blue paint. Some of the stores had striped canvas awnings. There was a barbershop with a red-and-white-striped barber pole and the usual hitching posts with an occasional water trough.

Though it wasn't St. Louis, Violet felt giddy just being in town. She hadn't slept very well the night before, worrying about Tangleweed and what to say to Lance once the place was sold. She wanted go there by herself; then she would sell Tangleweed to Ralph Nolan, if he still wanted it, considering what had happened the previous day.

For now, Violet had other things on her mind: for starters, meeting Velma Campton. After resigning herself to the fact that she had to follow Ruth about town while supplies were being bought and ordered, she planned what she would say to Mrs. Campton.

They went into the general store where she discovered that a letter from her Aunt Tilly had been waiting for her. Reading it quickly proved her resolve of the previous night. Her mother was still faring badly and was extremely upset by the news of Hattie's death. She insisted that Violet come home as soon as possible. Violet tucked the letter into her worsted bag, deciding there was little she could do at this point. She had already written a letter to her mother regarding her plans, which she mailed at the store. It was best not to worry. That's what her mother always said she should do under trying circumstances, and this was, without a doubt, a trying circumstance.

It was getting close to eleven o'clock when Ruth and Violet started toward the buggy. Ruth was unable to keep up with Violet's quick pace. In nearly every store they had entered, someone remarked about the "up-and-comin' weddin'." At first, Violet smiled, simply stating that a mistake had been made and that there would be no wedding. Her words seemed to go unnoticed as dozens of questions were asked about the "joyous occasion." Violet had to remind herself not to get angry. After all, Lance had apologized. She hoped all the gossip would die down soon.

That was her solace until one portly, elderly woman had followed them into the mercantile, huffed right up to the counter and, after demanding to be waited upon, looked up at Violet and shook her bonneted head disdainfully. "In all my days," the woman declared, "I've never known of any decent young lady agreein' to marry a man she'd never even met. It's brazen, if you ask me." The woman then plopped her worsted bag on the counter. "What's this world comin' to?"

Upset, Violet pursed her lips, refusing to say anything. She turned and stormed out of the store with Ruth close behind. Not wanting to discuss what had just happened, Violet insistently assured Ruth that she would discuss the matter with Lance later. If they tarried any longer they would arrive late to Velma Campton's, who lived across town.

* * *

The ride across town helped to calm Violet's nerves, although it did not settle them completely. Ruth stopped the buggy in front of Velma's small, white house with delicate lattice work at the roof peaks and around the front porch. Off to the side, a turret reached skyward, and a dormer could be seen spouting from the rooftop. From the moment Ruth pulled back the reigns, she could tell Violet was impressed by what she saw, causing her to sigh in relief.

Soft, sweet fragrances drifted out to greet them from the flowering vines covering the trellis shading the front porch and from the arbor near the side of the house. Ruth thought being there might be a pleasant diversion for Violet, possibly reminding her of home and her mother, which, hopefully, would take her mind off scolding Lance the next chance she got. To Violet, it was like walking into a picture book.

With both ladies breathing a bit easier, they followed the cobblestone walk to the door. Ruth rapped lightly, and they were promptly invited inside by a small, precise-looking woman who was dressed in a soft rose-colored dress made of printed challis. Her tawny curls were swept into a soft knot and held in place with tortoiseshell combs.

The green brocade curtains were drawn against the day's heat, so the house was cool when they stepped inside. The earthy smell of rich, green ferns and sun-drenched rugs intermingled with the aroma of freshly baked cookies. Violet nodded a polite "how do you do," after which they were escorted into the parlor.

Velma Campton offered Violet and Ruth a place to sit then left the room, returning shortly with a tray holding a pitcher of lemonade and a china plate piled with cookies. Again, she made a hasty retreat, her skirt rustling over the floor.

Violet smiled in awe of her surroundings. She was delighted to find such and extraordinary woman living in a little town hewn from the wilds of Texas. She heard a twittering noise and noticed a parakeet in a cage near one of the windows. Everywhere she looked, there were polished tables with delicate bric-a-brac on starched doilies. She admired a small footstool worked in fine needlepoint and the multicolored area rug that appeared to have been hand-braided.

Violet's thoughts were interrupted when Velma walked through the door carrying a silver tray loaded with sliced sweet bread and thick wedges of chocolate cake with pink icing, along with fancy glasses full of chipped ice.

"My!" Ruth exclaimed. "Looks like ya' might'a been expectin' us!"

Velma set the tray down and motioned for the ladies to help themselves.

"I figured you'd be coming into town soon. I had a notion you'd be anxious to show off the future bride."

Ruth nearly choked on her lemonade. She flashed a sidelong glance at Violet, whose back shot up straight like a rattlesnake ready to strike.

Violet cleared her throat. "I understand there's been some rumor going around about my marrying Mrs. Tridel's nephew, but I assure you it's all been a mistake."

No one spoke for a few seconds. Ruth's expression was one of uncertainty. She had hoped that when Violet went to get the cows, Lance had lived up to all his boasting. She squirmed against the back of the horsehair sofa.

"To tell ya' the truth, they hardly know each other," she said, as though Violet wasn't present.

Velma pursed her lips. "Well, Lance shouldn't go and get our hopes up that way."

"You know how he is," Ruth said, shaking her head from side to side. "Give 'em some time, and who knows what' ll become of it."

Violet, sure she saw Ruth wink at the woman sitting across from her, cleared her throat as she bent to set her glass on the tray. "Well, actually I came here to . . ."

"We all know what you came here for, honey, and we're real sorry about your pa." Velma set down her plate and looked straight into Violet's blank face. "But you can't fret forever over what's happened to him. You have to get on with your life, just like the rest of us."

Velma looked at Ruth, her brows bent in question. "Don't you think they'd make a nice pair, though?"

Ruth could tell Violet was getting angry as she began to fidget. "Well, I reckon only time will tell," she said quickly, glad to have the last word. She hurriedly changed the subject.

"We've sure been havin' a lot of rain lately. Ben and the boys are fixin' to round up a herd O' mustangs up at Silver Springs, just in case there's any floodin' out that way."

"Is that so?" Velma asked inquisitively.

"I was wondering, Mrs. Campton," Violet interrupted in a precise, lady-like manner. "I understand you've done some alterations for Mr. Thurman."

Velma's neck stiffened and she quickly swallowed her lemonade. Dabbing her mouth with her napkin, she inclined her head toward Violet. "He stopped by a time or two."

Violet pretended to look surprised. At least she had gotten the woman's attention. "Mrs. Tridel and I visited with the Thurmans. From . . ."

Velma turned her attention to Ruth. "That was terrible about his boy dyin' and all."

"From what I hear," Violet continued, "Mr. Thurman can't say enough kind things about all you've done for him since his wife died."

Velma gasped into her napkin just as Ruth set her plate down with a clatter. Folding her hands abruptly in her lap she refused to look at Violet.

"In my opinion," Violet proceeded undauntedly, "any man who is as devoted as Mr. Thurman is to his children deserves a good, caring woman. Why, if the right woman came along, she could fix that place up beautifully."

The parakeet squawked and fluttered loudly against the sides of the cage, but the commotion went unnoticed.

Violet caught a quick breath, her attention fixed on both women who stared at her with their mouths gaping. "In St. Louis, a woman with your capabilities would jump at the chance to have such a caring man call on her." Reaching for her bag, she stood up. "But then, it's my understanding you weren't interested in having a gentleman caller."

Violet briefly paused, smoothing out the wrinkles on her skirt while Velma squirmed in her chair. "I don't suppose you would mind if I talked to him about tutoring his daughter Lindsey in the evenings. I've been told you need a schoolteacher in Wood River. I'm sure Mr. Thurman is a member of the school board. Once he sees what an excellent instructor I am, I'm sure he'll vote to hire me."

Stopping abruptly, Violet looked up, a canny smile lighting up her face. "You know, now that I think about it, with a little touching up here and there, Mr. Thurman would be a very handsome man. Why, back in St. Louis, some of the most refined and prominent men in the community are much older than he is."

Violet set her shoulders in conclusion and extended an eager hand. "You don't know what an opportunity this is for me, Mrs. Campton. I've always wanted to go to some out-of-the-way place and help those in need." After shaking Velma's hand, Violet started briskly across the room. Ruth stumbled to her feet and followed Violet, her mind preoccupied on wondering what Violet was up to.

"Don't bother to see us out. It's much too hot outside for you to be standing in the sun," Violet said, as she and Ruth walked toward the front door, their skirts rustling. "Good—bye Mrs. Campton, and thank you ever so much for your hospitality." The two women hustled out of the house, letting the door click shut behind them.

*   *   *

"Of all the bold-faced lies!" Ruth blurted after they were in the buggy and had driven a safe distance from the house.

"I wouldn't go so far as to call it a lie," Violet stated coyly. "I just might decide to ask Mr. Thurman about tutoring Lindsey. And as far as what I said about him admiring her work, well I'm sure someone's said that about her at some time. As a matter of fact, I think you said he hated to have her leave. After all, she appears to be quite talented."

"But why'd you have to go and make him out like some sort of ladies' man when he ain't no such thing? You never even seen the man. He's as gangly as a willow tree and hairy as a he-goat."

Grinning from ear to ear, her lashes fluttering lightly, Violet replied, "That's not what Velma Campton thinks."

"Well, if that don't beat all," Ruth said, shaking her head in disbelief.

The ride home seemed to have calmed Violet's anger, until Lance helped her out of the buggy when they reached the Rough and Tumble. He no sooner set her down on the ground when she whirled around and swung at him.

Throwing back his head he groaned. "Now what was that for?" He looked over at his aunt, who helplessly shook her head and started off toward the house. Mumbling to herself, she said, "At this rate, they ain't never gonna get together."

"All morning I've been gawked at, talked about, told I was brazen, and treated like a suspect involved in some sort of crime. Maybe next time,

Mr. Lance Tridel, you should think twice before you decide to include me in your ill humor—and in your future!"

Violet stomped off toward the house, and Lance stormed off in the direction of the barn. Neither one came to the table for supper that night.

The next day, Violet felt ashamed of her hasty behavior. Still, she couldn't force herself to confront Lance. She pleaded a headache as an excuse to leave the room every time someone mentioned his name. If he came striding into the yard and she happened to be in the garden hoeing, she slipped into the tool shed; or, if she was in the house and she heard the back door slam shut, she would quickly hide in the pantry, making sure he never caught sight of her.

But when the men came riding in from the roundup about sundown the following day, a thundering cloud of dust rolling behind them like a cyclone, she watched anxiously from her bedroom window until she caught sight of Lance's white stallion with the patch of black around his right eye. With great prowess and a lot of hooting and hollering, the men rode hard and fast, cutting the horses toward the corral. Lance, who was in the lead, was sitting straight and tall in his saddle, his face partially hidden by his wide-brimmed hat and a lasso ready in his hand should one of the horses try to break free of his command. He pushed his hat back, and Violet saw the determination that fired him as he drove the herd of mustangs into the corral. Suddenly, she knew she loved him and that someday, if Lance felt the same way, Wood River, Texas, would be her home.

That night, Violet cried herself to sleep when she thought how foolish she had been. After the tongue-lashing she had given him, Lance would probably never speak to her or look at her again. She probably meant nothing to him, nothing but a passing whim, like having a dancehall girl fix him up a lunch. She wouldn't blame him. Her eyes swelled with tears and her lips trembled when she thought of his comforting embrace the night when they watched the sun set like a jewel on the meadow, the same night he had told her about his parents. She loved him, but there was nothing she could do about it now.

During the week, Lance watched playfully as Violet scurried about the yard or up the stairs to her room in order to avoid him. He smiled to himself and joked with Ruth about their cat-and-mouse game, reminding his aunt that in the end the cat always won.

Lance snatched a glance at Violet every night at supper, flashing her a wink when their eyes happened to meet. Violet's face would turn as pink as a new, sun-blushed apple, and she'd fumble with her fork, or take a quick sip of water, in an attempt to dismiss his attention. Later, Ruth would scold Lance, telling him what a "good-for-nothin' rascal" he was. Nonetheless, Ruth smiled fondly at him when his face perked up, the way she knew it would when Lance would peck her on the cheek then push open the screen door, calling over his shoulder that it just brought back memories of her courting days.

*   *   *

The last days of June slipped by unnoticed. On the day before the picnic, Ruth sent Violet up to the attic for some tick pillows she wanted to give to the Thurmans. After Violet had brought them downstairs, Ruth began tearing them open so she could wash and bake the feathers. She then realized she had forgotten to have Violet bring down the new ticking packed away in the attic. Happy to have something to do to keep herself occupied, Violet hastened up the stairs and was diligently searching through one of the trunks when she heard someone coming up the stairs. Without turning around, she knew that it was Lance standing in the stairwell.

"I thought I might find you up here," he said in a slow, even voice.

Violet turned around, her arms surrounding the ticking. "I was just looking for . . ."

"I didn't come up here to talk about pillows," Lance said. "You've been avoidin' me all week. I figured the only way I was gonna get to say what was on my mind was if I caught ya' where ya' couldn't run from me."

A warm rush swept through Violet, leaving her weak kneed and trembling. "I . . . I wanted to say I was sorry, but . . ."

"I got what was comin' to me. I'll have to watch what I say in the future. But I reckon if I can handle a herd of wild mustangs, I can learn how to deal with that temper of yours."

Violet glanced at Lance. It was hard to make out his expression, though, since he was standing in the shadows. "It was my fault from the start," she stammered. "I mean, I shouldn't have tried to slap you the way I did, without talking to you first. But Hattie told me . . ."

75

"What's the difference of talkin' first and then wallopin' or wallopin' first and then talkin'? If ya' don't mind, I'd like to know which way it's gonna be so when we get married, I'll know what to expect when I come walkin' through the door at night."

There was a moment of silence before Violet meekly replied, "You mean you really do want to marry me?"

Lance stepped up into the attic, shuffling through the scattered odds and ends until he reached her. Encircling her in his arms, he kissed the top of her head and softly uttered, "I don't know any other way for ya' to become Violet Tridel, unless ya' wait for Aunt Ruth to die and ya' marry Uncle Ben."

Violet stepped back, wiping tears from her lashes so she could see Lance's face. A look of uncertainty was etched along his brow until, with the tips of her fingers, Violet smoothed away the lines. She slipped her hands into his and whispered, "I've been wondering what it would be like being married to a cowpuncher."

Lance cupped Violet's face in his wide calloused hands, and she reached up and met his kiss.

Feeling taller than the sky, Lance returned to the stables, flashing a conquering smile at Ruth, who was bent over the washing.

With a feeling of warmth and contentment welling up inside of her, Violet started down the stairs when suddenly she realized that she had forgotten to tell Lance about her plans to sell Tangleweed. She didn't want them to live there, because of what had happened to her father. She would remember to tell him tomorrow, after the picnic.

There was an engagement celebration at the Rough and Tumble that night. Ruth made fried chicken and her famous chocolate cake, a meal she usually fixed on Sundays. When she set the table, she put out her fine china teapot, a gift from her mother when she got married. A fruit jar of bluebonnets set off a white embroidered tablecloth. She also made a pitcher of sassafras tea, adding a few sprigs of mint leaves for color.

Everyone dressed up for the occasion. Violet wore her blue-sprigged muslin dress with a white sash. Lance had on his favorite shirt, the color of midnight blue, and had polished his boots. Ruth and Ben had taken their time putting on their Sunday best.

After supper, the hired hands moved the table against the wall, and Ben took out his harmonica and whipped up a few tunes. The men crowded around the dining room, stomping and clapping along with the music.

Their eyes never wavered from the young couple who tirelessly danced in the center of the room, their feet never seeming to touch the floor. The doctor stopped by to see how Violet was getting along, and he promptly joined the festivities. The celebration went on past midnight with none of the men retiring until he'd had a chance to dance with the bride-to—be.

It wasn't until after she had gone to bed that Violet wondered how she was going to tell her mother she was marrying a cowboy and settling down in Texas. There was no getting around it. The wedding would have to wait until her mother was well. Violet would have to make arrangements to go back home as soon as possible.

Chapter Eight

The next morning, Violet opened her eyes as soon as the first sprinkling of sunlight slipped between the parted curtains. She was wide awake, too full of happiness to sleep any longer. Rolling over on her side, she hugged her knees to her chest that was full of a feeling of giddiness. Violet hadn't realized her heart had been crying out for someone special to love. She had the desire to laugh, sing, and dance; there didn't seem to be room for common, everyday things. She felt beautiful, full of every good and wonderful wish her heart had ever desired. She sprang from the bed, tossing the pillow aside and whirling around the room, holding her gown out at her sides. Then, with a feeling of lightheartedness, she flopped back on the bed, stifling an uncontrollable desire to laugh.

She was about to pull her gown over her head when she heard tapping sounds on the windowpane, as if someone was throwing pebbles. Ecstatically, she flew toward the window and promptly drew back the curtain. Lance was looking up at her, his face vibrant in the faint morning light. When he smiled Violet thought how handsome he was and how happy he looked.

Lance called up to her: "Hurry and get dressed, and we'll go riding before breakfast. I have a surprise for you."

Violet looked toward the stable and saw that he had saddled Shiner and another horse. She smiled at him. "I'll only be a minute."

"Hurry or I'll leave without ya'," he teased.

Violet let go of the curtain and rushed to the armoire in search of something to wear. Throwing off her gown, she pulled out her favorite fawn-colored riding habit and quickly got dressed. She swiftly tied her hair back. There was no time to fix it up properly. She could almost hear her mother scolding her as she flew down the stairs and out the front door.

Lance was there with open arms to greet her, kissing her in the shade of the honeysuckle vine. Hand in hand, they ran across the yard. He lifted her up into the saddle and then swiftly mounted his horse, calling over his shoulder for her to follow him.

They were nearly down the length of Old Dicey road when Lance pulled sharply on his reins and waited until Violet's horse came to a standstill beside him. Lance's horse tugged at the bit, tossing his shaggy mane and snorting, eager to keep moving.

Violet secured her reins and leaned forward into the saddle horn, laughing and out of breath. "Thanks for waiting for me. I was beginning to wonder if we'd make it up that hill."

"Looks like ya' did all right to me."

Violet smiled. "I never thought I'd find myself out riding with a man at the break of dawn, charging across the wilds of Texas."

"Any regrets?" Lance eyed her from beneath the rim of his Stetson.

"Only that I didn't do it sooner," Violet said taking a deep breath. "It's all so exhilarating and beautiful! Just look at the sky. Don't you just love how wide and free it is?"

Lance smiled, happy to see Violet so smitten by the beauty of the country he loved. Feeling overcome by her enthusiasm, and yet finding himself unable to express the way he felt, he looked up at the horizon and replied in a simple, offhanded fashion. "Looks like we might be in for some more rain. Aunt Ruth's sure gonna be put out."

"I'd love to ride in the rain," Violet said with eager anticipation.

"I can tell you've never been caught in a Texas cloudburst."

"What's a little cloudburst?"

Lance tipped his hat back slightly and shook his head with a frown. "Around here they come up faster than ya' can bat an eye, and it rains so hard the roads and creeks are washed out in a matter of minutes."

Violet looked at the sparsely scattered clouds, laced with wisps of gray and faint rays of sunlight, and laughed. "I'll keep that in mind should I ever find myself caught in one."

"If you're out riding, the best thing to do is to stay on your horse. It's the safest place to be."

"Well, you have nothing to worry about. Back in St. Louis, I'm considered to be an excellent horsewoman."

Lance sat back in his saddle and took up his reins. "Is that a fact? Let's just see how . . ."

His words were cut off by Violet's swift departure as she whipped her horse into an instant gait and sailed across the rocky terrain. Lance charged after her, whooping and hollering as though they were in a cross-country race and nearing the finish line. In a matter of minutes, he was gaining on her, leaning close to Shiner's long, sleek neck. Lance's legs hugged the horse's sides as if his life depended on it. Soon they were riding side by side at breakneck speed, with each horse's mane standing straight back and their hooves pounding the ground.

Lance caught Violet's eye as he slipped past her, motioning toward a clump of trees in the distance until he was sure she understood they were to stop there. She caught his meaning and snapped her reins, letting out a screech that sent her horse whizzing past him toward their destination. Her horse's tail was straight in the wind, and his legs seemed permanently bent with speed like lightning, his thundering hooves barely touching the ground.

When Violet reached the outer edge of the trees, she abruptly pulled on the reins, causing her horse to rise upright and paw the air before clattering to a standstill. Moments later, Lance came skidding to a halt beside her, his face filled with relief.

"You never told me ya' could ride like that."

Trying to catch her breath, Violet laughed. "I usually don't go around bragging about my achievements."

"Anyone would have thought you'd been racin' across Tangleweed country all your life."

Violet caught her breath. "You mean . . ."

"I told ya' I had a surprise for ya'. We've been ridin' on your land now for close to half an hour."

"It's . . . so beautiful . . . so . . . ." She stopped, unable to describe how she felt.

Pleased with himself and with the outcome he had expected, Lance smiled and told Violet he would show her where her father had panned for gold.

Violet rode her horse at a slow pace. She absorbed the impact of where she was. Her heart swelled with an overwhelming desire to reach out and become a part of every bit of this piece of earth. She had intended to tell Lance about her plans to sell Tangleweed, now she knew she couldn't follow through with her plans.

Everything Violet saw had belonged to her father. She believed the hills appeared as they did and the rain-washed flowers blossomed because he intended for them to be that way. A cool breeze washed over Violet's face, then slid through her hair. She felt at peace with herself and with her father. He had left her something after all. Tangleweed would forever be a reminder of what he stood for.

After Lance showed Violet where her father was buried, they explored several of the surrounding trails that seemed like caverns tunneling through the trees. They stopped by a trickling brook, sparkling with the sunlight that dotted the treetops, and drank from their cupped hands. Lying back on a bed of soft, cool moss, they talked about their childhoods while listening to the quiet sounds of the woods. Before they left the clearing, Lance cradled Violet against him and whispered to her of his loneliness before she came. When he told her he was afraid of losing her, she stroked his lean face, browned by the sun, and kissed him softly, promising never to leave him.

Lance and Violet went back to her father's cabin where they sorted through her father's belongings. It was close to ten o'clock when Lance suggested they head for home. Violet took one last look at the cabin's sleepy windows partially hidden by creepers, and the knobby chimney that was beginning to crumble. She told herself the place needed her care.

They rode side by side, sharing quiet conversation. Lance talked about what he was planning to do with the mustangs then Violet talked about her father.

"I wonder if anything will ever be done about my father's murderer," she muttered, her words weighted with concern.

"The sheriff has some leads, so I'm sure something will come about soon," Lance replied. A moment of silence passed, Violet thinking about Lance's response while Lance's thoughts had turned toward their wedding.

"How would ya' feel about gettin' married before the end of summer?"

Violet smiled at the look of concern still lining Lance's brow. "I should go home until my mother is feeling better," she answered.

Lance nodded. Nothing was decided upon; it wasn't a day for making decisions.

*   *   *

Ben and Ruth were just climbing into the wagon when Lance and Violet rode into the yard.

"So, how'd ya' like Tangleweed?" Ruth called out to Violet, her eyes smiling.

Violet looked surprised. "How did you know we went to Tangleweed?"

Ruth chuckled. "I reckon after ya' raised a boy all these years, ya' just get to where ya' can kinda guess what he's up to."

Violet looked at Lance, who was leaning casually on his saddle horn, his hands crossed at his wrists. His gray eyes were steady, and he looked like a man who knew what he was all about. Violet felt warm inside, knowing she would someday be able to say things like that about him and maybe even about a child of theirs. She wrapped her reins around the pommel of her saddle and eyed the loaded wagon.

"I guess we're more than a little bit late. I'll hurry and change and be down in a minute."

Ruth quickly raised her hand in protest. "There ain't no time for that, honey. Ya' look just fine the way ya' are."

"But, my hair." Violet's hand slid over her windblown hair. "I don't even have a bonnet on. And I really should change out of my riding habit."

"If ya' figured ya' looked good enough for Lance, then ya' look good enough for any of the folks that'll be over at Thurman's place."

"Ya' look fine to me," Ben added.

Violet couldn't help but shake her head and smile fondly at Ben. She could tell by the look on his scrubbed and shaven face that he didn't like dressing up. He was plainly dressed in a white shirt and black trousers, his shoulders bent slightly under a pair of new suspenders. His hair was slicked down and combed back in place, and his white brow was creased where his hat brim usually rested on his tanned face.

"Thank you, Ben," she said. "I'm beginning to think I can always count on you to help me make up my mind."

Ben's head swayed to one side and he growled. "You two better follow us. There ain't much room left in the wagon."

As their horses plodded slowly down the road toward the Thurmans' Violet could tell that Ruth was talking about the beauty of the countryside. Every so often she would nudge Ben until he looked to where she was pointing. Violet was content riding beside Lance while feeling the swaying of the horse and the wind in her hair. Still, she had never gone to a social gathering without properly dressing up, and she was worried she might appear out of place. When they approached the Thurmans', however, her uneasiness vanished. She noticed several women without bonnets, most wearing simple day dresses without frills and lace. Nobody wore the customary gloves her Aunt Tilly always insisted were necessary for social occasions. Violet sighed, knowing she would have felt rather foolish had she worn what she had originally planned. Living in Wood River would take some getting used to.

The wagon stopped in front of the house, and several young men immediately came to help unload the food. Ruth warned them with a stern, though gentle look not to sample any of the food before it was time to eat.

Violet followed Lance to the barn. A few of the horses had been unsaddled and tethered to a rail fence surrounding part of the yard. Lance dismounted swiftly and lifted Violet off her horse, his hold lingering on her waist after he had set her on the ground. Glancing around the yard first, Lance drew Violet to the side of the barn and lifting her face to his he then kissed her. Violet reluctantly wriggled out of his embrace.

"Someone will see us," she whispered loudly.

Lance looked at her with adoration in his eyes. "I hope the whole world sees us," he said, raising his voice.

"They will if you don't let go of me, Lance Tridel, and then you'll have to talk mighty fast to get yourself out of this one."

"And what makes ya' think, little lady, that I want to get outta this one?" Lance let go of her waist, caught her by the wrist, and promptly drew her along behind him as he started toward the house. "It's high time everyone in Wood River knew we're fixin' to get married for real."

Violet pulled back, unable to control her nervous laughter. "I'll be embarrassed," she cried between efforts to catch her breath.

"No ya' won't. If ya' don't come now, I'll tell all the ladies you're a real schoolmarm, and they'll be trailin' ya' around all day with a whole passel of kids tryin' to get ya' to help them fix up the schoolhouse, and . . ."

"You wouldn't!" Violet objected firmly.

"Well, maybe not, 'cause then they'd be followin' me around all day, too. But I will kiss ya', right here in front of everyone if ya' don't stop playin' hard to get."

All at once, Violet seemed more than willing to be led by Lance to the group of people who had eagerly gathered upon hearing the commotion coming from the direction of the barn.

"You're going to pay for this, Lance Tridel," Violet chided under her breath.

"Is that a promise?" Lance shot back. "If so, I'll be sure and hold ya' to it."

"Ohhh!" Violet groaned between her teeth. "You're insufferable," she added before she appeared from behind Lance wearing her prettiest makeshift smile.

"Friends and relatives of Wood River," Lance began, once he was sure that he had everyone's attention, "we're all here today because of the sorrow that has befallen the Thurmans . . ."

Violet looked puzzled. She wondered what Lance was going to say. She looked up at him and was touched by the feeling lining his face.

"We all loved Joey like he was family," Lance continued, "and there's nothin' sadder than losin' someone we love. But it would be a sorry thing if we let grief swallow us up, takin' away what we've been tryin' so hard to become all our lives. So, no disrespect intended, Abe." Lance nodded briefly at Mr. Thurman, "but I want to share some happiness with everyone here today, hopin' when we go home tonight we'll take some joy with us and not feelin's of regret and sorrow."

Lance paused for Mr. Thurman's nod of approval which he gave, and, for a shaky moment, Violet wondered if Lance was doing the right thing. The look on Lance's face was the same as when he had told Violet about the deaths of his parents. Several of the women were dabbing their eyes and sniffing quietly. Ben made a rattling sound when he cleared his throat just before Lance continued speaking.

"I want everyone here to know I've asked Miss Violet Tippon to marry me, and she's agreed to be my wife."

The crowd was still. Everyone's eyes appeared empty. Violet, who could barely see through her proud blur of tears, was afraid that Lance had gone too far. Then suddenly, Mr. Thurman, who was spruced up and standing like a young sapling beside Velma Campton, started to clap. Soon everyone was clapping, their voices buzzing with enthusiasm. The women rushed toward Violet until she was hemmed in by an assorted array of flouncing skirts. All of them tried to hug her at once, pressing their tear-stained cheeks to hers. The men slapped Lance on the back and bellowed, "It's about time someone made an honest man outta you, Tridel."

The bustling crowd lingered for a long time, asking all sorts of questions about the wedding, where Lance and Violet were going to live, and what kind of gown Violet was going to wear. They continued talking until the wind started to pick up slightly. The men decided to put up a makeshift shelter to keep things dry for the picnic in case it started raining. Arm and arm, the women walked toward the house.

* * *

Once inside, chairs were set in a semicircle around the living room so the women could begin cutting squares and piecing them together for the quilt. The windows were opened just enough to let in a nice, stiff breeze. Already, some of the older women who didn't have children to tend to were settling in comfortably and stitching squares together, their nimble fingers weaving their needles as fast as the gossip that flew between them.

When Violet entered the room, Velma Campton was the first to rush toward her, her hands busily fumbling at a broach pinned to her high-necked blouse.

"Since you'll be staying in Wood River, I was wondering if you might like to display a few of your bonnets in my store," she said primly.

Violet hesitated. "Well, I . . ."

"I saw the bonnet you gave Lindsey. It's simply beautiful. It must be the latest style in St. Louis."

"Yes, it is," Violet replied cordially.

"Then you must come and work for me in the store. Your bonnets will sell like hot cakes."

"Oh my!" one of the ladies gasped before someone else quickly exclaimed, "wouldn't that be excitin', Wood River havin' its own milliner?" All of the ladies started talking at once, the exuberance in their voices sounding like the drone of bees.

"Actually," Violet's voice rose above the steady hum, "I wouldn't mind displaying my bonnets, but I think I would like to make them at home."

A look of alarm flashed over Velma's face. "I was considering hiring a girl for the lunch hour. I always close the store and go home for lunch. But if you were there, the ladies could come in and choose . . ."

Velma abruptly stopped talking, a broad smile crowning her lips when she saw Violet's face light up.

"What about having Mr. Thurman's daughter, Lindsey come in then?" Violet suggested, causing Velma's smile to wane. "I'm sure she would love to have some time to herself. After displaying the fabrics and the notions she could write down the orders. I'd be willing to train her on her first day."

"Why, I never thought about Lindsey," Velma said, looking pleased. "I could talk to her father and . . ." Velma's head bent to one side and she dropped her lashes modestly. " . . . and see if something might be arranged. She raised her head, her lashes guarding the careful look in her eyes. "For such a young girl, she has an awful lot to do at home."

All the ladies agreed, their heads nodding in unison, their chatter taking on the sound of droning bees.

"This would be the perfect time to talk to Abe," Velma said in a sure voice before she turned and flounced out the door.

Violet was certain that Velma's seeing Lindsey every day would give Velma the opportunity she needed to get to know Mr. Thurman better. She smiled, feeling quite pleased with herself. Crossing the room, Violet sat beside a fragile-looking woman who didn't appear to be much older than herself. She was dressed in a loose-fitting, calico dress, and she had long, sandy-colored hair that was braided and hanging to one side of her softly featured face. Violet picked up a pair of scissors and an old shirt that had belonged to Joey and started cutting out squares.

"My name's Billy Jo," the woman said in a slow, kind voice. "My husband, Frank, and I live on a small place just off Windmill Road, between here and Bartlett."

Violet smiled shakily. "I'm afraid I don't know where Windmill Road is," she replied, pausing before she added, "but I did come through Bartlett on my way to Wood River."

Billy Jo's reassuring smile made Violet feel at ease. "You'll get used to things 'round here once ya' been here a while. It took me a while 'fore I stopped gettin' lost every time I went to town; but now I can just about find my way blindfolded. I lived in Bartlett when I met Frank at a dance one winter. We got married that summer. Once in a while, I kinda wish we could live back in Bartlett, but Frank has work here and he don't care to pick up and move."

A prickly chill ran up Violet's spine. She thought she could forget about what had happened in Bartlett, but the mention of the town filled her with apprehension. No one said anything about what the sheriff was going to do about her father's killer. And after someone had already tried to kill her twice, she wondered if staying in Texas would put her life in further danger. Violet suddenly realized that she wasn't paying attention to what Billy Jo was saying.

"I'm sorry. What did you say?"

"Oh, it was nothin'. I can remember doin' a lot of day dreamin' like that 'fore Frank and I was married. Ya' better do it now, cause after the youngins' start comin', there ain't no time for such things."

"It sounds like you have a family," Violet said.

Billy Jo gave a quick nod. "We got three, two boys and a girl, and one on the way."

"When are you expecting?"

"Some time in August."

"I'm sure Mr. Thurman appreciates your coming here to help out."

"We wouldn't think of not comin'. Poor Abe's had a hard time of it."

"I heard about his wife and how Joey had been sick for so long." Violet paused, her hands still for a moment. "I hope all that's behind him now and he'll find some happiness." She gently bit her lower lip, thinking how she had decided that today would be for her, too—a day to remember her father by. For some reason, Violet was afraid to ask the question that was on the tip of her tongue. But there was so much she still wanted to know.

"Did you know my father?" The words seemed to blurt out of her mouth.

Billy Jo nodded, a smile forming on her lips while she continued snipping the seams on the nightshirt she was cutting for the quilt. "Everyone in these parts knew ol' Tippon."

Violet stopped cutting squares and laid the scissors on her lap. "What was he like?" she pleaded softly, bending slightly toward Billy Jo, until it appeared Billy Jo felt compelled to look at her.

"He was the kindest man a body could know. He always came 'round to take my boys fishin', and there wasn't a time he didn't try to drag Frank away from his chores so he could go along, too. He liked to hunt some, and in the winter, when rations were gettin' low, why, he'd show up with a bunch'a rabbits or some squirrel, or sometimes deer meat."

She stopped talking and Violet saw her eyes blink rapidly. "I'm sorry," Violet said, placing a comforting hand on her knee. "I didn't mean to make you sad. Remember, Lance said we should be happy today."

"Oh, I'm just that way. Any little ol' thing can start me to cryin'."

Violet smiled kindly. "Well, I'm glad to know you. Thank you for telling me about my father." She stood up. "I think I'll go find Lance."

Violet placed the tattered shirt and the squares, along with the scissors, on the chair where she had been sitting and started across the room, nodding slightly and forcing herself to smile at the women, their eyes full of curiosity as they watched her leave. Once she was outside, she took a deep breath and let it out slowly. She felt as though she had been holding her breath for a long time.

Violet had been afraid that if she asked Billy Jo about her father, Billy Jo might ask her why her father and mother had separated or tell her something she didn't want to hear—something dreadful, such as the stories she used to fabricate in her mind as a child after her father had gone away. Instead, Billy Jo had been kind and obliging, sharing fond memories that made her cry. None of the ladies Violet knew in St. Louis would dare confess to having known a worn-out, old man who brought rabbits to their back door as a kindness, or cry in front of her because they missed him now that he was gone.

"Is somethin' wrong, Miss Tippon?"

Violet lifted her eyes and met Ben's face, which was lined with worry. She batted her lashes and sniffed back the urge to cry. "I was just wondering if my father ever talked about me?"

"Now, what brought this on?"

Violet shrugged. "Today—what everyone's doing here for Mr. Thurman."

Ben patted her on the shoulder. "Why, sure he talked about ya'." His voice perked up. "He told us what ya' looked like when you was born and how when ya' was just a little bit of a kid, you liked gittin' all fixed up so you could go paradin' down the walk with your doll buggy."

"Why didn't he ever write to me? All those years I thought he was dead."

Ben's Adam's apple slid up and down his neck as he gulped. "I . . . I reckon he was ashamed o' what he did . . . leavin' ya' behind and all."

"I would've forgiven him long ago if only . . ."

"Folks ain't got no way o' knowin' that. All they got inside of 'em is naggin' doubts and fears, so they stay away a little longer just livin' off the fond memories. Then 'fore they know it, years've gone by and it's too late to go back."

Violet stood quietly on the porch step, working her fingers as if she was braiding her hair.

"You gonna be all right?" Ben asked in a low voice.

Violet nodded. "Thank you. I guess being here today just made me think of what it could have been like if only . . ."

"Miss Tippon!"

Violet looked up and saw the man who owned the general store walking toward her.

"I figured you might be here today," he said, "so I brought along this letter. It arrived this morning."

"Thank you," Violet said, smiling.

As the man started to walk away, he turned and added, "Oh, by the way, congratulations."

Violet lifted her chin in acknowledgment. "Thank you."

"That letter 's probably from your ma," Ben said. "I'll leave you to read it by yourself, that is if you're sure you're gonna be okay."

Violet smiled at Ben and, without further pause, slipped the letter into her pocket and started walking toward the springhouse. If she had a few moments alone, she knew she would feel better. She had no sooner started down the footpath when someone called her name. She turned around and saw Lindsey walking toward her with a tall, lanky boy at her side.

"Lindsey, I was wondering where you were."

Lindsey lowered her eyes and laced her fingers together at her waist. "I just wanted you to meet Jed. We was engaged to be married 'fore Ma died."

"Nice to meet ya', Miss Tippon," Jed said.

"I've been wanting to meet you too, Jed." Violet's face softened at the look of tenderness on their faces. "I hope you'll be able to get married soon."

With a resigned look on her face, Lindsey shook her head, releasing a deep, uneven breath. "I guess now with Joey dyin' and all, Pa will be needin' me till he starts to feelin' better."

Jed took Lindsey's hand and held it tightly. Then, reaching out and touching Lindsey's shoulder, Violet smiled affectionately at her. "It won't be long, Lindsey, you'll see. By the way, have you talked to Mrs. Campton yet?"

Lindsey shook her head.

"She has a surprise for you, something that might hurry along your wedding plans."

"Velma Campton?"

Violet nodded. "I think she's inside helping some of the ladies get tables ready since it looks like it's going to rain."

"Thank you, Miss Tippon," Lindsey cried. Jed nodded in Violet's direction, and they hurried off toward the house, leaving Violet free to make her way to the springhouse.

Chapter Nine

O nce she made certain she was alone, Violet slipped behind the building and sat on the grass in the cool shade. She took out the letter that was addressed in her Aunt Tilly's familiar handwriting, tore open the seal, and began to read. An immense feeling of disbelief engulfed her. Her mother was dead. Reading on through a veil of tears Violet learned that her mother's condition had taken a turn for the worse, and there had been nothing more the doctor could do.

The words blurred on the paper, their meaning throbbing in Violet's head in quick, disjointed pictures. Everything around her seemed to vanish—the breeze stirring in the treetops, the scurrying sound of animals fleeing the coming rain. She felt herself falling into the dark purple funnel swirling behind her eyes. Feeling weightless, Violet fell sideways into the grass. Her numbed thoughts were interrupted by the muffled sound of men's voices coming from inside the springhouse. She heard her own weak voice cry out for Lance before she realized it wasn't Lance's voice she had heard. It was Ralph Nolan's. He was talking to someone who was bragging about some gold he had taken from Tangleweed.

"At least you're managing to get that right," Nolan said. "So far, you've messed up twice on getting rid of the girl."

"I did what ya' told me to do," a rough voice growled back at him.

"How do I know you're going to do it right this time?" Nolan jeered.

"I reckon third time's the charm."

The man's wicked laugh made Violet cringe. She clutched her stomach, forcing herself not to move. She suddenly recognized his voice; it was the man who had kidnapped her near Bartlett.

"If you would have shot her like I told you to, instead of dumping her in the middle of the road, this whole mess would have been cleared up by now, and Tangleweed would be mine, the way it was meant to be in the first place."

"I thought I could scare her off."

"Well, she doesn't scare off too easily, does she? You messed up again when I took her out to Tangleweed."

"I wasn't countin' on Tridel trailin' ya'."

"Well, get it straight this time. Remember, this is your last chance."

A slow, rumbling thunder crawled overhead, and the sky grew dim. Violet remained motionless, her entire body cramped with pain.

"It looks like it's going to rain, so everyone's busy taking stuff inside," Nolan continued. "They won't miss us if we head out to Tangleweed now. You can show me where you found the gold, and then I'll come back here. You hide out along Green Acre Road until Lance and the girl head for home. And if you have to, get rid of Tridel, too."

Violet didn't realize she had fainted until a raindrop splattered on her cheek and she opened her eyes. She dragged her weary frame up against the side of the springhouse, careful not to make a sound. The last thing she remembered was hearing the springhouse door shut and the sound of footsteps fading rapidly. She started when Nolan's terrifying secret flashed through her mind, making her too aware of her desperate plight.

Nolan had hired someone to kill her tonight!

She had to find Lance. She had to tell him that it was Ralph Nolan who had killed her father and who had tried to kill her, and that now he and his partner were heading out to Tangleweed to steal her gold.

But she still needed proof. She decided that if she followed Nolan and caught him stealing gold from her father's claim, it would be all the proof anyone would need.

Trembling with anticipation, Violet was afraid to move—afraid that someone would see her as she headed toward the barn. Her legs weak and her knees shaking, she crept along the wall, moving slowly at first, until she felt certain she could make it along the path unnoticed. She was halfway up the footpath when she saw a boy coming out of the stable. Running to him, she ordered the boy, in a hurried, almost frantic voice, to bring out her horse.

The boy looked up at the heavy gray clouds. In a careful voice, he said, "But it's fixin' to rain, ma'am. You sure you want to go out now?"

"I'll be back before it starts raining hard." Not wanting to be seen, she pushed ahead of the boy into the stable and urged him to hurry. She knew it would be raining soon, and she feared she would lose her way if the sky grew any darker. The boy led her to the stall where her horse was standing beside Shiner. With a look of despair on her face, she quickly surveyed the stable. "Is there a side door I can use?"

The boy frowned, pointing across the barn to where the door was. "Is anything wrong, Miss Tippon?" he asked.

Violet wanted to cry out that her mother died, that she was being hunted down like an animal, that there was a chance she might not make it through the night alive. But she only managed to shake her head, paying little attention to the worried expression on the boy's face.

Seeing some bridles hanging on a nail beside the stall, Violet grabbed one and slipped it over the horse's head, shakily working the bit into the horse's mouth.

"Don't ya' want me to saddle your horse?"

"No," Violet replied. Without saying another word, she led the horse out of the stall and through the side door, wondering as she did so if she was doing the right thing in not telling Lance where she was going. Violet decided there was no time to search for him, or to answer questions. It would be raining soon. She feared she would lose her way if the sky grew any darker. She was numbed to reason, driven by despair and the desire to catch Nolan and his accomplice before they got away with the gold. She wanted the satisfaction of being a witness against Nolan herself.

Violet turned and looked at the boy's solemn face. "Don't say anything to anyone, unless Lance should come looking for me. Only then can you tell him that I went to Tangleweed."

The boy nodded hesitantly as he watched Violet climb onto the horse's bare back and quickly disappear into the trees that lead away from Thurman's house. She drew the reins to the south, and at the same time realized she would be totally defenseless if she were spotted by Nolan or his hired man. Pulling back on the reins, she stopped for a moment to take a deep breath and gather the needed courage to proceed alone.

* * *

A half hour went by before Lance realized he hadn't seen Violet for some time. A soft, steady rain was falling, and thunder rolled overhead, filling him with apprehension. He had searched the house and the yard, asking everyone he saw if they had seen Violet. No one remembered seeing her from the time they had all been in the yard.

Lance wasn't overly worried until he talked to Ben, who told him that he thought Violet seemed upset when he had last seen her heading toward the springhouse. Lance frowned, knowing he had already checked there. Borrowing Abe Thurman's greatcoat, Lance strode across the yard toward the barn, the only place he hadn't looked. He pulled his hat down to keep the rain off his face. When he looked up, Tommy Combs, the boy tending to the horses, was running toward him.

"Are you lookin' for Miss Tippon?" Tommy asked.

"Yeah, do you know where she's at?"

The boy huddled inside his shirt to keep the rain off his head. "She told me not to say anything unless ya' was to ask after her. Then she said to tell ya' that she was headin' out to Tangleweed."

"Tangleweed! Why would she go there?"

"She didn't say."

Lance threw his head back until rain was spitting at his face. "Was it raining when she left?"

"It was just startin' up."

Lance grabbed the boy by the arm, shaking him roughly. "Why'd you wait till now to tell me? You know it's not safe to be riding in those hills in the rain."

Tommy winced at Lance's scowling face and let out a cry as he tried to jerk from his strong grip. "She said she'd be back before it started rainin'."

Lance groaned angrily and released the boy, who ran quickly toward the house. Lance wondered why Violet would go to Tangleweed and not tell him. Confused, he stormed into the barn. The rain was growing heavier and the thunder boomed as it slowly crept southward. After a few moments, horse and rider charged out of the barn, the sound of hooves pounding the sodden earth, echoing upward and fading into the storm. With Lance's head pressed low against Shiner's neck, they bolted down the road toward Tangleweed.

*   *   *

Drenched and discouraged, the thrill of pursuit having left her, Violet knew she was a fool to have started out alone. The rain increased, making it difficult to see what lay ahead. She feared she was lost, and it was all she could do to keep from giving in to despair. She reminded herself, even as she guided her horse along the narrow footpath, that there was no way she could turn back now.

After her horse plodded up a steep incline, she noticed the road ahead was full of loose stones. Afraid her horse might stumble and send them both tumbling into the brush at the foot of the hill, she decided to dismount and lead her horse through the rocky pass. In the leaden sky overhead, the clouds gathered ominously, reminding her of the lightning bolt that had struck the tree along the road to Bartlett.

A cold wave of terror flashed through her, abruptly causing her to be still. Her cry was muffled by the sound of growling thunder. She dropped the reins, choking back a sob while clutching the horse's sodden mane and burying her face against his neck to calm her fears. She realized that every move could be her last, and that she might never see Lance again.

She struggled against an overwhelming feeling of loneliness. Yet somewhere deep inside of her, she knew that no matter what happened, she owed it to her father to go on. Wanting more than anything to see Ralph Nolan behind bars, she took a deep breath and continued, ready to confront Nolan.

After walking a short distance, looking for a sign that she was on the right track, she climbed onto the horse's back and started toward an abandoned hovel. It was the same one Lance had pointed out to her when they had gone to Tangleweed. Before she realized she was approaching her father's land, she heard an earth-shattering blast that shook the ground beneath her. She had heard that sound only once before, having seen crews of men working on the railroad in Missouri. She immediately knew it was the sound of exploding dynamite.

Keeping a steady grip on the reins, and carefully staying close to the underbrush along the swelling stream, she nudged her horse toward the bank where she could see two men on the opposite side, near her father's cabin. One of the men turned around and then quickly turned his back to her. Violet became worried, wondering if he had spotted her. She was pretty sure she was well-hidden by the heavy drizzle and the underbrush.

95

After a moment had passed, a flood of relief swept over her, and Violet coaxed her horse closer to the path that edged the stream. Brushing strands of wet hair from her face, she bent near the horse's neck and peered through the swaying tree branches. All at once, another blast startled her and she flew backwards. Her horse snorted loudly and stamped his hooves. It took all of the strength she could manage to calm him. When she peered once again through the trees, the sight that met her eyes made her gasp. The side of the hill that had been blown away was laced throughout with strands of glimmering gold. Caught between feelings of astonishment and utter confusion, she failed to notice that the men were nowhere in sight. When she came to her senses, her first thought was one of imminent danger; she had to get away before it was too late.

Just then, the sky opened wide and rain poured in sheets from the black, rumbling clouds. Violet struggled to back her horse away from the bulging stream when a bullet whizzed by her, searing a deep path along her arm that burnt like liquid fire. She let out a piercing scream, dropped the reins, and grabbed the throbbing stream of pain on her arm. The horse blew a mean protest through his flared nostrils, rearing with his massive hooves pawing the air until Violet went tumbling backward into the stream that had now become a raging river.

Her cries were washed away by the slapping torrents that swiftly carried her downstream. Violet thrashed against the wind and pelting rain as she slipped deeper into the muddy rapids that she feared would soon become her grave. She fought the churning waters, gasping and panting until she was thrown violently against a fallen tree. The painful jolt blinded her for a clenching moment. Clawing frantically at one of the tree's branches, she willed herself to live. She shouted to the dark figure of a man on horseback near the edge of the bank, but her cries faltered in the slashing rain.

Ralph Nolan's sordid laugh reached her ears. "There's no one here to save you this time, Miss Tippon. Good-bye. Thank you for making me a rich man."

Violet's shrill scream for help penetrated the roaring stream, and when Nolan turned to leave, she dropped her head onto the bobbing tree limb and let out a wretched cry. Weighed down by her soaked riding habit, she felt defeated. She grew rapidly weaker as swell after swell of murky water sprayed her face, leaving her breathless and unable to gather the strength, or courage she needed to fight her way back to the bank. When she thought she could no longer cling to the tree limb, she peered into the storm and saw herself running hand in hand with Lance through a bright field covered with bluebonnets. She was wearing a long, flowing dress with a veil that was caught up in the wind. On her finger there was a gold band that glittered as it caught the sun's rays. All at once, Lance was gone. Violet cried out, realizing she, too, had disappeared. She called for Lance, shouting for him to come back when she saw a figure on horseback emerging from the trees just beyond her father's cabin.

*   *   *

Huddled low in the drenched coat, his head bent under his dripping hat, Lance cradled the loosened reins in his hand, allowing his horse to pick a path along the underbrush. He was relieved to know that he had at last approached the clearing near Tippon's cabin. He stopped for a moment to listen to the fast-moving rapids and the thunder that rolled above the treetops. He frowned in frustration, straining to hear what he thought was the sound of someone crying for help. But the slashing rain cut the cries in two. He bent his head into the wind and cautiously angled his horse along the crooked path that followed a band of trees down the cascading hillside.

Lance had nearly made it to the foot of the hill when he heard the piteous cry again. This time he knew it was Violet. Then he saw her, laboring against the torrents in the middle of the bulging stream. He cupped his hands to his mouth and shouted into the wind.

"Violet! hold on! Don't let go!"

He snapped up the reins and whipped his horse around, spurring him to the water's edge while he reached behind him, to the back of his saddle to grab a rope. Quickly knotting it into a lasso, he secured the other end of the rope to his saddle horn and began spinning the loop above his head. Suddenly, a bullet cut his cheek as it whizzed by him, sending a ready flow of warm blood streaming down his face. Stunned, Lance's hold on the rope loosened, and it fell into his lap. His face tightened with pain. In one rapid sweep he scanned the hills. It wasn't until then that he saw the side of the hill that was blown away and the gold veins glistening through the rain. A feeling of utter disbelief rushed through him that left him feeling paralyzed. Then, suddenly, he was distracted by a swift movement. He whipped his head around just as a man darted from behind the cabin into the thicket. A shot rang out and a scream cut through the onslaught of rain, jolting Lance to his senses. There was no time to think. In one swift move, he whirled the lasso and flung it into the stream. The loop caught a notch on the limb that Violet clung to.

"Violet! Grab the rope!" he shouted. Anxiously, he watched Violet struggle against the tumbling peaks, frantically trying to reach the rope. "Now!" he demanded. But a huge swell caught her and threw her backward into the rapids where she disappeared. A moment later, she bobbed up, panting and gasping for air.

The cracking sound of gunfire rent apart the drumming rain. Without waiting another second, Lance jumped off his horse. He slapped a firm hand on Shiner's neck, commanding him to stay there. He gripped the rope, making sure it was taut; then, pulling off his hat, he plunged into the raging stream.

*   *   *

Nolan watched as Lance fought his way across the angry stream, laughing triumphantly when Lance stumbled and fell, barely able to keep his head above the rippling swells. He mounted his horse and jerked the reins to the side, coaxing his horse along the muddy trail. By morning Lance Tridel and Violet Tippon would merely be names on the lips of mourners, he thought to himself. Then, after staying away for a few days, he would casually drift into the Tin Star Saloon, where he was certain someone would eagerly relate the whole story to him. After that, he would ride out to the Rough and Tumble, offer his condolences, and walk away as the rightful owner of the Tangleweed Ranch.

Chapter Ten

*I*t was all Lance could do to keep a firm grip on the rope and fight the pounding waters while struggling to keep his head above the oncoming current. He shouted above the noise of the storm to Violet, who, although appearing exhausted, managed to cling to the tree limb. He hoped the sound of his voice would keep her holding on until he was able to reach her.

With the adrenaline rushing rapidly through his body, Lance plunged through the lashing stream toward Violet, grabbing her by the arm just before her hold weakened and she let go of the limb. Fear engulfed him. Violet's face was chalky white, her lips a pale blue color. He had no way of telling whether she was dead or alive. He cried out, not realizing it was the sound of his own misery that echoed above him. With his strong arm wrapped tightly around Violet's waist, Lance used every ounce of strength he had left to force his way through the rapid currents until he felt the rocky bottom beneath his feet. He caught the tangled brush along the bank and he pulled himself and Violet to higher ground where they both collapsed in exhaustion.

The rain pelted Lance's face with unrelenting force while his chest heaved as he fought to catch his breath. He was unable to feel or move his limbs, aware of nothing but the pulsating rhythm that beat numbly throughout his entire body. Slowly and with effort, he rolled onto his side toward Violet, who, when he was able to focus his eyes on her, appeared to be dead. He let out a cry of alarm and struggled to his knees. Bending over her, he dropped his head to her breast and heard the faint sound of her beating heart. Without delay he swept her up, renewed strength pouring into him, and strode toward the cabin.

As Lance made his way to shelter, it occurred to him that Nolan had escaped. He was sure that once it stopped storming, however, Nolan would come back for the gold. Lance looked at the hills knowing that any road that would take him and Violet to safety would soon be washed out. His only hope was that the rain would let up and he could get Violet away before sunrise. He looked down at her blue-tinged face, and desperation gripped him. He vowed between clenched teeth to catch up with Nolan if it was the last thing he did.

When he reached the cabin, he kicked open the door, walked toward the bed, and gently laid Violet on the worn feather-tick mattress. He tore off his coat, and without pausing, removed her soaked clothing. Realizing she had been shot, he muttered an angry curse and bandaged her arm with a strip torn from her petticoat. After wrapping her in a blanket he had taken from his saddlebag and covering her with his greatcoat, he brushed aside wet strands of hair that clung to her ashen face then rubbed warmth into her hands.

Hesitant to leave her side, Lance made a fire from some brushwood and twigs he gathered from the floor of the lean-to. Then he hurried to undress himself, draping his clothes over some chairs he set in front of the fire. He wrapped himself in a rough blanket he'd found in a pile of old clothes. The chilling effect of the stream stayed with him until he was finally dressed in his dry clothes, the warmth beginning to penetrate his skin. After his teeth stopped chattering, and feeling somewhat hopeful, he quietly searched the cupboards until he found a small can of sardines and a can of beans.

"Ain't like Aunt Ruth's cookin', but it'll have to do," he said under his breath as he pried off the lids with his pocketknife. After he had warmed up the food, he sat next to the bed, his rifle cocked and leaning against the wall, while he ate his meager portion and waited for Violet to wake up. The color had returned to her lips and her face no longer appeared ashen, but Lance was still afraid she would not make it till morning.

The battering rain continued without letup, pouring from the roof in sheets that masked the windows. Lance dozed in a chair, waking to rekindle the fire when he felt chilled by the wind that swept down the chimney and whistled through the cracks in the walls. He used what was left of the wood in the lean-to and then was forced to burn the furniture to keep the room warm throughout the night. Once the fire was again crackling, he sat back down, peering worriedly at Violet's face before he settled back into his chair and quickly dropped off to sleep.

*　　*　　*

The sun's rays were just beginning to slip beneath the door and the cracks near the boarded windows when Violet awoke the next morning to the sound of someone cranking water at the well. Every muscle in her body cried out in pain as she dragged herself up against the bedstead, wondering where she was. The door opened slowly and Lance towered in the doorway.

"I remember seeing you standing in a sunlit doorway when I first came to Texas," Violet said weakly.

"Some things never change," Lance said, stepping inside and kicking the door shut with his foot. "Have any regrets?"

"Only that I wish we'd met sooner."

"Well, there's always ways to make up for lost time, but right now all I care about is gettin' you outta here before Nolan comes back."

"You think he'll come back so soon?"

"I'm sure he thinks we're dead. Besides, I never knew a man yet who'd turn and run from gold."

Violet's eyes drifted as they took on a dazed look. "That gold was the most beautiful sight I'd ever seen."

Lance plunked the bucket on the table. "Having a gold mine in your backyard would tend to make you a bit starry-eyed."

Violet tried to draw her knees up but found she was too sore and stiff. "If only my father could have lived to see it," she said, sighing.

"I think he was just as happy knowing it was there," Lance replied, moving toward the bed. Their eyes met. "Are you going to be all right?" he asked. Violet nodded, and Lance sat on the edge of the bed and tenderly stroked her bruised face. "I thought I was going to lose you, Violet."

"I should have . . ."

Lance touched her lips with his fingertips. "Remember, no regrets," he said before he kissed her softly, then stood up and went to the door where he turned to look back at Violet. "The horses are ready to go. There's no time to waste. Your clothes are on the bed, and I left a few sardines and some beans there on a plate for you. Call me when you're ready." Lance stepped into the light of early dawn and shut the door with a thud.

Violet didn't realize how weak and hungry she was until she tried to get up from the bed and a purple swirl spun through her head. She sat back down, her hand over her closed eyes, until the dizziness passed. Then, with slow, precise movements, she dressed herself as quickly as she could. She picked up the tin plate of food and nearly fainted from the smell before she dropped it and hurried out the door.

Before the sun had fully peaked, Lance and Violet were headed back to the Rough and Tumble. Lance had tied the reins of Violet's horse to his saddle horn, and holding Violet protectively against his chest, they inched their way along the mucky trail home.

*   *   *

Violet stayed in bed the following week with chills and a fever that left her feeling weak and depressed. She had recurring nightmares in which she was being pursued by Ralph Nolan. Wearing a black mask over his face he charged after her on an enormous, black steed. No matter how fast she ran, she never lost sight of him, the sound of his horse's hoof beats pounded against her temples until the pain was unbearable. In front of her, the road ended suddenly and she felt herself falling, tumbling headlong into a great ocean until she landed with a splash that sprayed a fountain of gold dust skyward. She gasped, awed by its beauty before she realized that she was sinking deeper and deeper into the depths of the churning waters. Then she would scream and open her eyes, fighting the hands that sought to restrain her. As the fever lessened, Violet began to gain back her strength. Still, Ruth continued wringing her hands in her apron. Though Violet seemed grateful for all her care, she refused to be comforted, not even wanting to hear about the sheriff's efforts to search for Nolan or his shooter. One or two of the hired hands brought a handful of flowers. They all made an effort to keep quiet and not stomp across the floor when they would leave. One afternoon, Billy Jo brought Violet a sampler to embroider. She also showed Violet the baby gown she had been adding tatting to. Jed and Lindsey came for a visit, but when Ruth told Violet she had visitors, Violet simply turned her head away and refused to see anyone.

Sitting around the table that night after supper, Lance lamented. "She seemed all right when I brought her back from Tangleweed."

Ruth placed a comforting hand on his back and patted it tenderly. "The poor girl's had a hard time of it, Lance. Why, ever since she got to Texas, Nolan's been tryin' to kill her."

"The sheriff's doin' the best he can, but no one's seen Nolan since he slipped outta the saloon yesterday after hearin' you and Violet was still alive." Ben paused before expounding. "No one hides his tracks better than a wanted man."

"Ya' sure had us worried, Lance, stayin' gone all night and all," Ruth said, brushing a tear from her rounded cheek.

Ben cupped his bristled jaw and shook his head. "I think they had plenty o' worries of their own, what with a couple of vultures holdin' out in them hills."

"I couldn't send word or I would have," Lance explained.

"I know," Ruth said wearily as she shuffled into the kitchen. When she returned Ben and Lance were still sitting at the table, their heads hanging as if they were afraid that leaving the room might bring on another bout of misfortune. Without saying a word, Ruth set a pot of coffee, two mugs and two slices of pie on the table then went back into the kitchen. She made a pot of tea and set it on a tray next to a plate of cookies she had placed on a starched doily.

Lance took the tray up to Violet. He was pleased to see that she was up and had dressed herself in a cheery blue and white calico dress. She shook her head when he offered her the tray, so he set it on the nightstand and sat down next to her.

Violet was careful not to look at Lance. She kept her head down, looking at her hands cupped in her lap. "I've been doing a lot of thinking since what happened to us at Tangleweed, and . . ."

Lance's mind went blank, the sound of Violet's voice ringing in his head like the dull sound of a blacksmith's hammer striking an anvil.

"I . . . I've decided I can't live here anymore."

There was a painful penetrating silence before Lance spoke in a controlled voice. "We can live somewhere else then."

Violet looked up. "I don't want to feel guilty for the rest of my life because I took you away from all that you love. Lance, I . . . I just need to go back home."

Lance's jaw twitched as he fought to keep it from trembling. "But what about us?" He looked longingly at Violet. "You're all that I love, Violet. I don't want you to go. You promised you'd never leave me."

Violet's eyes filled with tears, and a bitter lump rose in her throat so that she was unable to talk for a moment. "I owe you my life, Lance. I'll never forget that. But . . . so much has happened here. When I got on the train in St. Louis, all I could think about was seeing my father. I never dreamed Hattie would die and I would be left alone in a shabby hotel, or that I would be sought after by desperate outlaws who wanted me dead." She raised her sorrowful eyes. "And I never expected to fall in love with Texas, or with you." She paused only long enough to see a tear land on her hand. "And my mother—I wasn't there when she needed me." Violet caught a sob in her throat, knowing that if Lance touched her she would lose her tottering resolve. "Please try to understand that I need some time to myself . . . time alone to think things out."

Lance understood losing someone to death, but he couldn't comprehend losing someone who was very much alive. Determined to make her stay, he placed his hands on her shoulders and gently turned her towards him. She began to sob, and Lance wiped the tears from her cheeks with his fingertips.

"You've changed since you've been here. It won't be the same if you go back now. You'll never be happy living the way you did back in St. Louis."

Violet looked into Lance's blue eyes clouded with worry, and she knew he was right. She dropped her lashes, keeping them tightly closed, trying to hold back the tears. She saw herself whirling in a cyclone of churning, muddy water, her screams rising above the booming thunder as she desperately struggled to grab the snagged tree limb. She could still see Nolan on the swelled banks watching her drown while his threat kept repeating itself over and over again in her mind. Her body began to shudder and then she fell limp against Lance, who quickly embraced her. Her weeping turned to racking sobs.

Violet knew that if she stayed it would be this way every day, like a ominous cloud hanging over her. Every night she would be afraid to be left alone. She would always be watching over her shoulder for Ralph Nolan, fearing what might happen to her if he or one of his men came back. With a suddenness, like that of striking lightening she was convinced that she must stick to her decision and leave before it was too late. She struggled out of Lance's desperate grip and looked up at the worried expression on his face. He would never be happy if someone tried to kill her again and he wasn't there to prevent it. It would be her fault if she didn't do something now. "I can't stay and live the rest of my life in fear," she concluded.

"We'll find Nolan, even if I have to go out and hunt for him by myself. I promise you, Violet he'll hang for what he's done. Just yesterday, someone saw him down at the Tin Star."

"And he got away, didn't he?" Violet remarked, sniffling and wiping her cheek with the back of her hand.

"He can't be far."

"I'm sorry, Lance. I love you, but I just can't stay here." She stood up, trying hard not to look at his face. "Please, don't be angry at me. It won't be forever, I promise."

"But when . . ."

"I've decided to take the stage in the morning and catch the train in Sander's Creek." Her voice cracked. "I'll ask Ben to take me." She walked to the door and reached for the knob, her head lowered. "I don't know when I'll be back." She hesitated.

"But how will I live without you?" Lance asked before she continued.

"I don't know," she wept. "Please say that you won't try to make me stay."

Without looking up, Lance said, "I promise." The door shut. Stunned, Lance sat motionless until he no longer heard Violet's footsteps. Then he stood up and walked to the window. He lifted the curtain just as Violet was running across the sunny meadow to the pasture where the cows had gone to graze. She was holding the hem of her dress in her hand as she seemed to disappear in the tall grass, like a wildflower being tossed by the wind.

*　　*　　*

The hot sun beat down until Lance's shirt was stained with sweat and clinging down the middle of his back. His turned up sleeves were wet from wiping his sweaty forehead. He pulled the posthole borer out of the ground and knocked the dirt off the blades with his boot. A hot, dry whiff of air stirred the dirt at his feet near the hole he was digging and spun a dust devil that leaped and then whirled away. He propped his elbow on the handle of the borer and arched the tight muscles in his back, wondering if he would feel better if he took off his shirt. His shoulders dropped. The effort seemed too much as down as he was feeling. Taking off his hat, he wiped his damp forearm across his brow then used his handkerchief to wipe the sweat from the band inside his hat. Then he fit the brim over his brow and paused for a moment to scan the heat waves that rippled on the horizon.

A dull surge of loneliness swept over him. He could picture the stagecoach leaving Wood River just after dawn on its way to the train depot in Sander's Creek. He heaved a disgruntled sigh and dropped his head. He'd been a fool to promise not to go after Violet. Maybe if he had gone after her, she would have changed her mind and stayed. Although he reminded himself that he'd always been a man of his word, he wondered now if that was as important as doing what felt right in his heart. Maybe this time being true to one's word wasn't as important as being chivalrous. Nonetheless he had made her a promise.

He cleared his throat, gripped the handle of the posthole borer, slammed the sharp wedges into the ground, and began to turn the dirt. He tried to picture Violet looking out the window of the narrow, swaying boxcar, watching the countryside fly by. He wondered what she was thinking about. His eyes started to tear as he remembered the state of disarray she had been in that day when they first met in the stagecoach. He hoped some other rambling cowboy wouldn't happen upon her and find her as lost and confused as he had. He comforted himself with the thought that she had told him that she loved him and would come back.

The faint sound of the dinner bell clanging met his ears and he figured he should head back to the house, even if he didn't feel like eating. If he didn't go in pretty soon, Aunt Ruth would send one of the hands out after him. He lowered his head until his shaded eyes were level with the fence line. Satisfied that it was straight enough, he dropped the posthole borer and started toward the creek, whistling lightly for Shiner to follow.

When he got to the edge of the creek, he rolled down his sleeves, then unbuttoned his shirt and peeled it off. He crouched at the bank and laid his shirt in the fast-flowing stream, holding it down by a large rock. He watched Shiner who was drinking deeply from the creek. After a moment, he pulled the shirt from the water, tightly wrung it out, shook out the wrinkles, and spread it flat on the grass to dry in the hot sun. He dropped down on his stomach and slid face first into the creek until the top half of his body was covered with the cool, gurgling water. Feeling refreshed, he lifted his head from the water and scooted back up the bank. He fell back on his knees and shook the water out of his glistening hair and with his open palms swept the water from his chest. Then he retrieved his nearly dry shirt.

He could still hear the resounding clang of the dinner bell as he stared beyond the swaying grass at a figure on horseback slowly approaching. He watched intently as he put on his shirt. The horse and rider drew closer. When the horse stopped, a woman wearing a straw hat and a long, flowing dress slid to the ground and started trudging through the tall grass. The sound of his heart grew louder in his ears, and everything around him seemed to fade except for the woman.

"Violet!" he cried, hesitating until he saw she had quickened her steps.

Calling his name, Violet pulled off her hat and waved it above her head so that he could see her face.

He started running toward her, and when they met he swept her up into his arms, holding her tightly against his chest, smothering her face and neck with eager, happy kisses.

"Don't ever leave me again," he demanded, feeling Violet's tears on his face. "I love you more than life itself."

"I love you, too. I could never leave you and be happy."

"What about . . . ?"

Violet placed her hand lightly on Lance's face, feeling his warmth and his strength. She closed her eyes. "1 can't be afraid forever. I know now that love is stronger than fear."

"I should've gone after you."

"I came back because you didn't."

Lance drew back, a look of wonder on his face. "What?"

"I knew you really loved me when I needed to leave and you let me go. You said I could go alone and you kept your promise. It wasn't until I had gotten on the stage that I realized you needed someone to trust and believe in, too, and that I had let you down."

"If what I'm feeling is disappointment, then let me down all you want," Lance said softly before he took Violet's face in his hands and kissed her lips tenderly. Then he took her hand in his and together they started across the grassy meadow. "We can build a house on the ridge overlooking the creek in front of your pa's cabin."

"And I'll plant flowers out front, and a vegetable garden. I've never planted a garden before."

"The kids will pick all your flowers," Lance laughed.

Violet giggled and flung her arms around Lance's neck, ruffling his hair until she broke away and started running down the slope. Lance ran after her and when he caught her, they tumbled through the wildflowers to the bottom of the hill. Holding her tightly in his arms, Lance brushed the hair from her face and kissed her again.

"Looks like I picked the most beautiful wildflower in all the state of Texas," Lance whispered in Violet's ear.

"And what do you intend to do with me now that you've picked me?" Violet teased.

"Show you off, like those city fellas do. And I'll say, 'this here's my bride, Mrs. Lance Tridel.'"

Violet added, "And I'll say, 'Here's the man I love more than anything else in all the world.'"

Lance stood up and drew Violet to her feet. Then he swept her up into his arms and started toward the house, a tall, proud cowboy carrying everything he'd ever wanted against his heart.